MOURNER AT THE DOOR

MOURNER AT THE DOOR

Gordon Lish

STORIES

FOUR WALLS EIGHT WINDOWS
NEW YORK / LONDON

PUBLISHED IN THE UNITED STATES BY
FOUR WALLS EIGHT WINDOWS
39 WEST 14TH STREET
NEW YORK, N.Y. 10011

U.K. OFFICES:
FOUR WALLS EIGHT WINDOWS/TURNAROUND
UNIT 3 OLYMPIA TRADING ESTATE
COBURG ROAD WOOD GREEN
LONDON N22 67Z

FIRST CLOTH EDITION PUBLISHED BY VIKING PENGUIN, INC. IN 1988. FIRST
PAPER EDITION PUBLISHED BY PENGUIN BOOKS IN 1989. FIRST FOUR
WALLS EIGHT WINDOWS REVISED PAPER EDITION PUBLISHED IN 1997.

LIBRARY OF CONGRESS CATALOGUING-IN-PUBLICATION DATA:
LISH, GORDON
MOURNER AT THE DOOR : STORIES/GORDON LISH
P. CM.
ISBN 1-56858-084-3 (PBK.)
I. TITLE.
PS3562.174M6   1997
813'.54—DC21   96-51153
CIP

PRINTED IN THE UNITED STATES
TEXT DESIGN BY INK, INC.
PRODUCTION BY MORGAN BRILLIANT
10 9 8 7 6 5 4 3 2 1

FOR BRODKEY, OZICK, DELILLO
AND TO JILLELLYN RILEY
AND FOR GARY LUTZ

. . . to keep a real and valued object in being.

—FRANK KERMODE

CONTENTS

It is reported that Wittgenstein's last words were these: "Tell them I have had a wonderful life." Perhaps he did and perhaps he did not—have a wonderful life. But how could Wittgenstein have known one way or the other? As to a further matter, suppose those were not the words—suppose the words were German words. What I want to know is this—is it the same thing to have a wonderful life in another language? Or put it this way—if another language was the language Wittgenstein had it in, then how could it have been a wonderful life?

MOURNER AT THE DOOR

THE DEATH OF ME

I WANTED TO BE AMAZING. I wanted to be so amazing. I had already been amazing up to a certain point. But I was tired of being at that point. I wanted to go past that point. I wanted to be more amazing than I had been up to that point. I wanted to do something which went beyond that point and which went beyond every other point and which people would look at and say that this was something which went beyond all other points and which no other boy would ever be able to go beyond, that I was the only boy who could, that I was the only one.

I was going to a day camp which was called the Peninsula Athletes Day Camp and which at the end of the summer had an all-campers, all-parents, all-sports field day which was made up of five different field events, and all of the campers had to take part in all five of all of the five different field events, and I was the winner in all five of the five different field events, I was the winner in every single field event, I came in first place in every one of the five different field events—so that the head of the camp and the camp counselors and the other campers and the other mothers and the other fathers and my mother and my father all saw that I was the best camper in the Peninsula Athletes Day Camp, the best in the short run and the best in the long run and the best in the high jump and the best in the broad jump and the best in the event which the Peninsula

Athletes Day Camp called the ball-throw, which was where you had to go up to a chalk line and then put your toe on the chalk line and not go over the chalk line and then go ahead and throw the ball as far as you could throw.

I did.

I won.

It was 1944 and I was ten years old and I was better than all of the other boys at that camp and probably all of the boys at any other camp and all of the boys everywhere else.

I felt more wonderful than I had ever felt. I felt so thrilled with myself. I felt like God was whispering things to me inside of my head to me. I felt like God was asking me for me to have a special secret with him or for me to have a secret arrangement with him and that I had better keep on listening to his secret recommendations to me inside of my head. I felt like God was telling me to realize that he had made me the most unusual member of the human race and that he was going to need for me to be ready for him for me to go to work for him at any minute for him on whatever thing he said.

They gave me a piece of stiff cloth which was in the shape of a shield and which was in the camp colors and which had five blue stars on it. They said that I was the only boy ever to get a shield with as many as that many stars on it. They said that it was unheard-of for any boy ever to get as many as that many stars on it. But I could already feel that I was forgetting what it felt like for somebody to do something which would get you a shield with as many as that many stars on it. I could feel myself forgetting and I could feel everybody else forgetting—even my mother and father and God forgetting. It was just a little while afterwards, but I could tell that everybody was already forgetting everything about it—that the head of the camp was and the camp counselors were and the other campers were and that the other mothers and the other fathers were and that my mother and my father were and that even that I myself was, even though I was trying with all of my might for me to be the one person who never would.

I felt like God was ashamed of me. I felt like God was sorry that I was the one which he had picked out and that he was getting ready for him to make a new choice and for him to choose another boy instead of me and that I had to hurry up before God did it, that I had to be quick about showing God that I could be just as amazing again as I used to be and that I could do something, do anything, else.

It was August.

I was feeling the strangest feeling that I have ever felt. I was standing there with my parents and with all of the people who had come there for the field day and I was feeling the strangest feeling which I have ever felt.

I felt like lying down on the field. I felt like killing all of the people. I felt like going to sleep and staying asleep until someone came and told me that my parents were dead and that I was all grown up and that there was a new God in heaven and that he liked me better than even than the old God had.

My parents kept asking me where did I want to go now and what did I want to do. My parents kept trying to get me to tell them where I thought we should all of us go now and what was the next thing for us as a family to do. My parents kept saying they wanted for me to be the one to make up my mind if we should all of us go someplace special now and what was the best thing for the family, as a family, to do. But I did not know what they meant—do, do, do?

My father took the shield away from me and held it in his hands and kept turning it over in his hands and kept looking at the shield in his hands and kept feeling the shield with his hands and kept saying that it was made of buckram and of felt. My father kept saying did we know that it was just something which they had put together out of buckram and of felt. My father kept saying that the shield was of a very nice quality of buckram and of felt but that we should make every effort for us not to ever get it wet because it would run all over itself, buckram and felt.

I did not know what to do.

I could tell my parents did not know what to do.

We just stood around with the people all around all going away to all of the vehicles that were going to take them to places and I could tell that we did not, as a family, know if it was time for us to go.

The head of the camp came over and said that he wanted to shake my hand again and to shake the hands of the people who were responsible for giving the Peninsula Athletes Day Camp such an outstanding young individual and such a talented young athlete as my mother and father had.

He shook my hand again.

It made me feel dizzy and nearly asleep.

I saw my mother and my father get their hands ready. I saw my father get the shield out of the hand that he thought he was going to need for him to have his hand ready to shake the hand of the head of the camp. I saw my mother take her purse and do the same thing. But the head of the camp just kept shaking my hand, and my mother and my father just kept saying thank you to him, and then the head of the camp let go of my hand and took my father's elbow with one hand and then touched my father on the shoulder with the other hand and then said that we were certainly the very finest of people, and then—he did this, he did this!—and then he went away.

MR. GOLDBAUM

PICTURE FLORIDA.

Picture Miami Beach, Florida.

Picture a shitty little apartment in a big crappy building where my mother, who is a person who is old, is going to have to go ahead and start getting used to her not being in the company of her husband anymore, not to mention not anymore being in that of anybody else who is her own flesh and blood anymore, the instant I and my sister can devise good enough alibis for us to hurry up and get the fuck out of here and go fly back up to the lives that we have been prosecuting for ourselves up in New York, this of course being before we were obliged to drop everything and get down here yesterday in time to ride along with the old woman in the limo which had been set up for her to take her to my dad's funeral.

It took her.

It took us and her.

Meaning me and my sister with her.

Then it took us right back here to where we have been sitting ever since we came back to sit ourselves down and wait for neighbors to come call—I am checking my watch—about nine billion minutes ago.

Picture nine minutes in this room.

Or just smell it, smell the room.

Picture the smell of where they lived when it was the both of them that lived, and then go ahead and picture her smelling to see if she can still smell him in it anymore.

I am going to give you the picture of how they walked—always together, never one without the other, her always the one in front, him always shuffling along behind, him with his hands always up on her shoulders, him always with his hands reaching up out to my mother like that, with his hands up on her shoulders like that, her always looking to me like she was walking him the way you would look if you were walking an imbecile, as if there was something wrong with the man, wrong with the way the man was—but there was nothing wrong with the way my father was—my father just liked to walk like that whenever my father went walking with my mother, and my father never went walking without my mother.

I mean, this is what they did, this is how they did it when I saw them, this is what I saw when I saw my parents get old whenever I went down to Florida and had to see my old parents walk.

Try picturing more minutes.

I think I must have told you that we made it on time.

Only it was not anything like what I had been picturing when I had sat myself down on the airplane and started keeping myself busy picturing the kind of funeral I was going to be seeing when I got down to Florida for the funeral my father was going to have.

Picture this.

It was just a rabbi that they had gone ahead and hired.

To my mind, the man was too young-looking and too good-looking. I kept thinking the man probably had me beat in both departments. I kept thinking how much the man was getting paid for this and would it come to more or would it come to less than my ticket down and ticket back.

I felt bigger than I had ever felt.

I did not know where the ashes were. I did not know how the burning was done. There were some things which I knew I did not know.

But I know that I still felt bigger than I had ever felt.

As for him, the rabbi took a position on one side of the room, the rabbi stood himself up on one side of the room, and me and my sister and my mother, we all went over to where we could tell we were supposed to go over to on the other side of the room, some of the time sitting and some of the time standing, but I cannot tell you how it was that we ever knew which one it was meet and right for us to do.

I heard: "Father of life, father of death."

I heard the rabbi say: "Father of life, father of death."

I heard the guy who was driving the limo say, "Get your mother's feet."

Picture us back in the limo again. Picture us stopping off at a delicatessen. Picture me and my mother sitting and waiting while my sister gets out and goes in to make sure they are going to send over exactly what it was we had ordered when she called up and called our order in.

Maybe it would help for you to picture things if I told you that what my mother has on her head is a wig of plastic hair that fits down over almost all of her ears.

It smells in here.

I can smell the smell of them in here.

And of every single one of the sandwiches that just came over from the delicatessen in here.

Now picture it like this—the stuff came hours ago and so far this is all that has come. I mean, the question is this—where are all of the neighbors which this death was supposed to have been ordered for?

I just suddenly realized that you might be interested in finding out what we finally decided on.

The answer is four corned beef on rye, four turkey on rye, three Jarlsberg and lettuce on whole wheat, and two low-salt tuna salad on bagel.

Now double it—because we are figuring strictly a half-sandwich apiece.

Here is some more local color.

The quiz programs are going off and the soap operas are coming on and my sister just got up and went to go lie down on my mother's bed and I can tell you that I would go and do the same if I was absolutely positive

that it would not be against my religion for me to do
it—because who knows what it could be against for you
to go lie down on your father's bed?—it could be some
kind of a curse on you that for the rest of your life it
would keep coming after you until, ha ha, just like him,
that's it, you're dead.

My mother says to me, "So tell me, sonny, you think
we got reason to be nervous about the coffee?"

My mother says to me, "So what do you think, sonny,
you think I should go make some extra coffee?"

My mother says to me, "I want for you to be honest
with me, sweetheart, you think we are taking too big of
a chance the coffee might not be more than plenty of
enough coffee?"

My mother says to me, "So what is it that is your
opinion, darling, is it your opinion that we could probably get away with it if your mother does not go put
on another pot of coffee?"

Nobody could have pictured that.

Nor have listened to no one calling us and no one
imploring us for us to hold everything, for us to keep
the coffee hot, that they are right this minute racing up
elevators and racing down stairways and rushing along
corridors and will be any second knocking at the door
because there is a new widow in the building and an old
man just plotzed.

You know what?

I do not think that you are going to have to picture anything along the lines of any of that.

Except for maybe Mr. Goldbaum.

Here is Mr. Goldbaum.

Mr. Goldbaum is the man who sticks his head in at the door which we left open for the company which was on the way over.

Here is Mr. Goldbaum talking.

"You got an assortment, or is it all fish?"

That was Mr. Goldbaum.

My mother says, "That was Mr. Goldbaum."

My mother says, "The Mr. Goldbaum from the building."

Now you can picture a whole different thing, a whole different place.

This time it's the Sunday afterwards.

So picture this time this—my sister and me the Sunday afterwards. Picture the two different cars we rented to get out from the city to Long Island to the cemetery. Picture the cars parked on different sides of the administration building which we are supposed to meet at for us to meet up with the rabbi who has been hired to say a service over the box which I am carrying of ashes.

Picture someone carrying ashes.

Not because I am the son but because the box is made out of something too heavy.

Now here is a picture you've had practice with.

Me and my sister waiting.

Picture my sister and me standing around where the offices are of the people who run the cemetery, which is a cemetery way out on Long Island in February.

I just suddenly had another thought which I just realized. What if your father was the kind of a father who was dying and he called you to him and he said you were his son and he said for you to come lie down on the bed with him so that he as your father could hold you and so that you as his son could hold him so that the both of you could both be like that hugging with each other like that for you to say good-bye to each other before you had to go actually go leave each other and you did it, you did it, you got down on the bed with your father and you got down up close to your father and you got your arms all around your father and your father was hugging you and you were hugging your father and there was one of you who could not stop it, who could not help it, but who just got a hard-on?

Or both did?

Picture that.

Not that I and my father ever hugged like that.

Here comes the next rabbi.

This rabbi is not such a young-looking rabbi, is not such a good-looking rabbi, is a rabbi who just looks like a rabbi who is cold from just coming in like a rabbi from outside with the weather.

The rabbi says to my sister, "You are the daughter of the departed?"

The rabbi says to me, "You are the son of the departed?"

The rabbi says to the box, "These are the mortal remains of the individual which is the deceased party?"

Maybe I should get you to picture the cemetery.

Because this is the cemetery where we all of us are getting buried in—wherever we die, even if in Florida.

I mean, our plot's here.

My family's is.

The rabbi says to us, "As we make our way to the gravesite, I trust that you will want to offer me a word or two about your father so that I might incorporate whatever ideas and thoughts you have into the service your mother called up and ordered, may God give this woman peace."

Okay, picture him and me and my sister all going back outside in February again all over again in February again and I am the only one who cannot get his gloves back on because of the box, because of the canister—because of the motherfucking urn—which is too heavy for me to handle without me holding onto it every single instant with both of my hands.

The hole.

The hole I am going to have to help you with.

The hole they dug up for my father is not what I would ever be able to picture in my mind if somebody came up to me and said to me for me to do my best to picture the hole they make for you when you go see your father's grave.

I mean, the hole was more like the hole which you would go dig for somebody if the job they had for you to do was to cover up a big covered dish.

Like for a casserole.

And that is not the half of it.

Because what makes it the half of it is the two cinder blocks which I can see are already down in it when I go to put down the urn down in it, the hole.

And as for the other half?

This is the two workmen who come over from somewhere I wasn't ready for anybody to come over from and who put down two more cinder blocks on top of what I just put in.

You know what I mean when I say cinder blocks?

I mean those gray blocks of gray cement or of gray concrete that when they refer to them they call them cinder blocks and they've got holes in them.

Four of those.

Whereas what I had always thought was that what they did with a grave was fill things back in it with what they took out.

Unless they had taken out cinder blocks out.

You can go ahead and relax now.

It is not necessary for you to lend yourself to any

further effort to create particularities that I myself was not competent to render.

Except it would be a tremendous help for me if you would do your best to listen for the different sets of bumps the different sets of tires make when we all three of us pass over the little speed bump that makes everybody go slow before coming into and going out of the cemetery my family is in.

Three cars, six sets of tires—that's six bumps, I count six bumps and a total of twenty-six half-sandwiches—six sounds of hard cold rubber in February of 1986.

Or hear this—the rabbi's hands as he rubs the wheel to warm the wheel where he has come to have the habit of keeping his grip in place on the wheel when—to steer, to steer—the rabbi puts his hands on the wheel and thinks:

"Jesus shat."

That's it.

I'm finished.

Except to inform you of the fact that I got back to the city not via the Queens Midtown Tunnel but via the Queensboro Bridge since with the bridge you beat the toll, that and the fact that I went right ahead and sat myself down and started trying to picture some of the things which I have just asked you for you to picture for me, that and the fact that I had to fill in for myself where the holes were sometimes too big for

anybody to get a good enough picture of them, the
point being to get something written, the point being
to get anything written, and then get paid for it, to get
paid for it as much as I could get paid for it, this to
cover the cost of Delta down and Delta back, Avis at
their Sunday rate, plus extra for liability and collision.

One last thing—which is that no one told me.

So I just took it for granted that where it was supposed to go was go down in between them.

THE MERRY CHASE

DON'T TELL ME. Do me a favor and let me guess. Be honest with me, tell the truth, don't make me laugh. Tell me, don't make me have to tell you, do I have to tell you that when you're hot you're hot, that when you're dead you're dead? Because you know what I know? I know you like I know myself, I know you like the back of my hand, I know you like a book, I know you inside out.

You know what?

I know you like you'll never know.

You think I don't know whereof I speak?

I know the day will come, the day will dawn.

Didn't I tell you you never know? Because I guarantee it, no one will dance a jig, no one will do a dance, no one will cater to you so fast or twiddle his thumbs or wait on you hand and foot.

You think they could care less?

But I could never get enough of it, I could never get enough. Look at me, I could take a bite out of it, I could eat it up alive. But you want to make a monkey out of me, don't you? You want me to talk myself blue in the face for you, beat my head against a brick wall for you, come running when you have the least little complaint. What am I, your slave? You won't be happy except over my dead body, will you? I promise you, one day you will sing a different tune.

But in the interim, first things first.

Because it won't kill you to do without, tomorrow is

another day, let me look at it, let me see it, there is no time like the present, let me kiss it and make it well.

Let me tell you something—everyone in the whole wide world should only have it half as good as you.

You know what this is? You want to know what this is? Because this is some deal, this is some setup, this is some joke. You could vomit from what a joke this is.

I want you to hear something, I want you to hear the unvarnished truth.

You know what you are?

That's what you are!

You sit, God forbid I shouldn't go—didn't I already have enough to choke a horse?

Go ahead and talk my arm off. Talk me deaf, dumb, and blind. Nobody is asking, nobody is talking, nobody wants to know. In all decency, in all honesty, in all candor, in all modesty, you have some gall, some nerve, and I mean it in all sincerity and truth.

The crust on you, my God!

I am telling you, I am pleading with you, I am down to you on bended knee to you—just don't get cute with me, just don't make any excuses to me—because in broad daylight, because in the dead of night, because at the crack of dawn.

You think the whole world is going to do a dance around you? No one is going to do a dance around you. No one even knows you are alive.

Just who do you think you are, coming in here like a lord and lording it all over us all? Do you think you are a law unto yourself? I am going to give you some advice. Don't flatter yourself, act your age, share and share alike.

Ages ago, years ago, so long ago I couldn't begin to remember, past history, ancient history—you don't want to know, another age, another life, another theory altogether. Don't ask. Don't even begin to ask. Don't make me any promises. Don't tell me one thing and go do another. Don't look at me like that. Look around yourself, for pity's sake. Don't you know one hand washes the other?

Take stock.

Talk sense.

Give me some credit for intelligence. Show me I'm not wasting my breath. Don't make me sick. You are making me sick. Why are you making me sick like this? Do you get pleasure from doing this to me? Why are you doing this to me? Do you derive satisfaction from doing this to me? Don't think I don't know what you are trying to do to me. You think you're so smart.

Don't make me do your thinking for you.

Shame on you, be ashamed of yourself, have you absolutely no shame?

Why must I always have to tell you?

Why must I always drop everything and come running just for me to tell you?

Does nothing ever occur to you?

Can't you see with your own two eyes?

You are your own worst enemy.

What's the sense of talking to you? I might as well talk to myself. Say something. Try to look like you've got a brain in your head. You think this is a picnic? This is no picnic. Don't stand on ceremony with me. The whole world is not going to step to your tune. I warn you, I'm warning you, don't say nobody didn't warn you—wake up before it's too late.

You know what?

A little birdie told me.

You know what?

You have got a lot to learn.

I can't hear myself talk. I can't hear myself think. I cannot remember from one minute to the next.

Why do I always have to tell you again and again?

Give me a minute to think.

Just let me catch my breath.

Don't you ever stop to ask?

I'm going to tell you something. I'm going to give you the benefit of my advice. How would you like it if I gave you some good advice?

You think the sun rises and sets on you, don't you? You should get down on your hands and knees and thank God. You should count your blessings. Why don't you look around yourself and really take a look at yourself for once, just for once in your life? You just don't know when you're well off, do you? You have no idea how the other half lives. You are as innocent as the day you were born. You should thank your lucky stars. You should try to make amends. You should do your best to put it all out of your mind. Worry never got anybody anywhere. Whatever you do, promise me this—chin up, buck up, keep an open mind.

What do I say to you, where do I start with you, how do I make myself heard with you? I don't know where to begin with you, I don't know where to start with you, I don't know how to impress upon you the importance of every single solitary word. Thank God I am alive to tell you, thank God I am here to tell you, thank God you've got someone to tell you, I only wish I could begin to tell you, if there were only some way someone could tell you, if only there were someone here to tell you, but you don't want to listen, you don't want to learn, you don't want to know, you don't want to help yourself, you just want to have it all your own way and go on as if nothing has changed. Who can talk to you? Can anyone talk to you? Nobody can talk to you. You don't want anybody to talk to you. So far as you are concerned, the whole wide world should keel over and drop dead.

You think it's all a picnic? Where did you get the idea it's all a picnic? Face facts, don't kid yourself, people are trying to talk some sense into you, it's not all just fun and fancy free, it's not all just high, wide, and handsome, it's not all just pretty is as pretty does.

You take the cake, you take my breath away—you are really one for the books. Be smart and play it down. Be smart and stay in the wings. Be smart and let somebody else carry the ball for a change.

You know what I've got to do?

I've got to talk to you like a Dutch uncle to you.

I've got to handle you with kid gloves.

Let me tell you something no one else would have the heart to tell you. You better look far and wide— because they are few and far between! Go ahead, go to the ends of the earth, go to the highest mountain, go to any lengths, because they won't lift a finger for you—or didn't you know some things are not for man to know, that there are some things that are better left unsaid, that there are some things you shouldn't wish on a dog—not on a bet, not on your life, not on nobody at all?

What do you want? You want the whole world to revolve around you, you want the whole world at your beck and call?

Be honest with me.

Answer me this one question.

How can you look me in the face?

Don't you dare act as if you didn't hear me. You want

to know what's wrong with you? This is what is wrong with you. You are going to the dogs, you are lying down with dogs, you are waking sleeping dogs—don't you know enough to go home before the last dog is dead?

When are you going to learn to leave well enough alone?

You know what you are?

Let me tell you what you are.

You are betwixt and between!

I'm on to you, I've got your number, I can see right through you—I am giving you fair warning, don't you dare try to sit there and put anything over on me or get on my good side or lead me a merry chase.

So who's going to do your dirty work for you?

Do me a favor and don't make me laugh!

Oh, sure, you think you can rise above it, you think you can live all your life with your head in the clouds in a cave like a hermit without rhyme or a reason, without a hitch, without batting an eyelash, without a leg for you to stand on, without one little bit of sugar on it and butter on your bread. But let me tell you something—you're all wet!

You know what?

You're trying to get away with it—with murder, with false pretenses, that's what!

You know what is wrong with you? I am here to tell you what is wrong with you. There is no happy medium

with you, there is no live and let live with you, there is
no by the same token with you—because talking to you
is like talking to a brick wall to you!

Pay attention to me!

You think I am talking just to hear myself talk?

SHIT

I LIKE TALKING ABOUT sitting on toilets. It shows up in the roughage of my speech. Wherever at all in keeping with things, I try to work it in. You just have to look back at stories I have had printed for you to see I am telling you the truth. Sitting on toilets is certain to show up with more than passing incidence. I will even go so far as to say that where you find a story with a person sitting on a toilet in it, forget the name that's signed as author—no one but I could have written the thing. Indeed, it would be inconceivable to me I didn't.

But the one I've got now, this one here, it promises to be the pick of the lot.

Or anyhow the purest.

Well, the truest, then—the least fictitious, then—then the one with not much in it made up.

The other thing about it that I like is that it could not be simpler for somebody to tell—nothing in it but just a man sitting on a toilet in it and the wallpaper in it the man is looking at.

Oh, of course—not just a man but myself.

How could I tell a story about anyone else? For one thing, it could never be true, could it? I mean, what do I know about people—or care to? Good Christ, I have all I can do to marshal even a small enough interest in guess who.

Or do I mean large enough?

I don't know.

THIS IS ANOTHER THING I am always putting into stories—"I don't know." Just those words, just like that. You see a story with "I don't know" in it, this'll be your tip-off as to who was it who wrote it. It could have anybody down there under the title there—but he isn't.

Or didn't.

It's exciting.

It is exciting.

Not writing, not speaking—but being a sneak.

When I was a boy, this was what I wanted to grow up to be—a person who was a sneak and an assassin. I wanted to be dangerous. This was when I was little.

When I was little, my mother would get me to sit on the toilet for her and stay there and stay there until I could show her something, and sometimes—more and more oftentimes—I couldn't. She would say, "Put your royal bombosity down on the royal throne and don't you dare let me see you get up off of it until there is something in there in it for your mother to look at."

It's terrible what I have to show for it now. I tell you, I don't know where the food goes. It's frightening. Am I getting poisoned? Or pickled?

I take things.

You know—to make me go.

I especially take things when we go away and it gets worse—not going, the not-going. This is where this comes in—the story, this story, the wallpaper. Listen to this—I had taken a lot of something—because it had been days already, days of nothing but of sitting and of not going already, of its maybe having been thus even for a week of it already. So I'd swallowed enough to choke a horse, gone to bed, been down for mere minutes, when I had to get back up again and I really mean it, what I said.

Get back up!

It was somewhere quaint—an inn somewhere—you lose track—a cute hotel—meaning no bathroom of your own, meaning a bathroom out at the end of the hall, meaning a bathroom with a kind of a latch contraption on the door—and with a pitched ceiling pitched so low you had to keep bent over—even sitting down, you had to keep bent down—and even bent, I couldn't stop going—oh, God, going and going. Forever it felt like.

Gallons it felt like.

It felt like my whole life was coming up and coming up—and going good and out.

I mean going down and out.

Which is when I started studying the wallpaper.

I thought I was sluicing away, dissolving from the inside out, rendering myself as waste, breaking down to basal substance, falling through the plumbing, perishing on a toilet I could not even call my own.

You'll laugh, but I got scared.

I thought: "Call for help."

I thought: "Do it before you swoon."

Which is when I reached out for the wallpaper as you would for a lifeline, for smelling salts, a float.

I don't know.

I thought: "Hang on to the wallpaper!"

I mean, with all my mind, with that.

Well, I could see it was a wallpaper you could do it with—a pattern—growing things—things that grow—a picture of this, then of that—and the names for them given as thus:

Blue-eyed grass.

Wintergreen.

Sweet William.

Sneezeweed.

Vetch.

Violet.

Primula.

Coreopsis.

Clover.

Mariposa.

Marsh marigold.

Rose mallow.

Dandelion.

Red-eye.

Clover.

Black-eyed Susan.

Poppy.

Bluebells.

Buttercup.

Hepatica.

Wood sorrell.

Belladonna.

Ivy.

I SWEAR IT—ALL THOSE, each and every one.

Grasses, weeds—I don't know—crap, all that itchy actual crap—pointless from the word go.

I sat there holding on.

For nothing less than for life itself.

Pretty dumb.

After all, all it was was just a lot of shit. If anything, I should have been joyous, been jubilant, been pleased as punch. Hey, come on—I was going, wasn't I?

But I was scared to death.

I thought: "Hey, hotshot, you think you're so smart, let's see you swindle your way out of this."

Skip it, what the tricks are—they are never not the plenitude the wallpaper-writer needs.

But ask yourself meanwhile this—which wallpaper-reader lived again to have for him to struggle again with shit like this?

RESURRECTION

THE BIG THING ABOUT THIS IS deciding what it's all about. I mean, by way of theme, what, what? Sure, it gives you the event that got me sworn off whiskey forever. But does this make it a tale of how a certain person got himself a good scare, put aside drunkenness, took up sobriety in high hopes of a permanent shift? I don't think so. Me, I keep feeling it's going to be more about Jews and Christians than about this thing of matching another man glass for glass. But I could be wrong in both connections. Maybe what this story is really getting at is something I'd be afraid to know any story I ever wrote is.

Either way or whatever, it happened last Easter, which doesn't mean a thing to me because of me being Jewish. To my wife it's something, though, and I am more or less willing to play along—providing things don't get too much out of hand. Egg hunts for the kids, this is okay, and maybe a chocolate bunny wrapped in colored tinfoil. But I draw the line when it comes to a whole done-up basket. I don't see why this is called for—strands of candy-store grass getting stuck between floorboards and you can't get the stuff up even with a tweezers or a Eureka.

As for the Easter that I am talking about, not much of all of this was ever at issue. This was because we got invited out to somebody's place. I think the question just got answered this way—whatever they do, this'll be it, this'll be Easter—no reason for us to have to make any decisions. Which was a relief, of course—the whys and the wherefores of which I am sure you do not need for me to turn nasty and explicate for you. But my wife and I, didn't we find something else for us to get into a fuss about, anyway? And this is the best I can do—say "something else." Because I don't remember what. Not that it was anything trifling. I'm certain it must have been something pretty substantial. I mean, aside from the whole routine thing of spouses with our differences doing Easter.

Our boy, however, he got us reasonably jolly just in time for our arrival. What happened was, you just caught it from him, his thrill at getting into all this country-ness of experience. You see, I think our boy really suffers in the city—I think my wife and I agree on this—not that you could ever actually get a confession of his unhappiness out of him. He's all stoic, this kid of ours—God knows from what sources. Twelve years old and tough as a stump, though to my mind a stump is nowhere near as tough as what I think you have to be as tough as. At any rate, he was out and gone as soon as we pulled up into the driveway. Trees, I guess, the trees. That boy, in him we're looking at a mighty delight to get up high on anything, his mother and his dad always hollering, "Come down from there! You're giving us heart trouble!"

The host and hostess, they were swell people. No need

to say more. Nice folks. I was going to say "for Christians," but it is never necessary for you to actually say it, is it? As for the houseguest thing, we can skip right from Friday when we got there to Saturday before supper, them having over a few neighbors to meet us—other couples, more Christians. There was this one fellow among them, he seemed to take me for a person of special interest. We got to talking with what was surely more gusto than you would have thought customary among such citizens. I don't know what about so much as I know it had to do with a lot of different municipal things—the houses around there, the gardening, getting the old estates up to scratch with strenuous renovations. There were these trays of Rob Roys going from hand to hand, and dishes of tiny asparagus spears and something lemony in a small porcelain bowl, kids underfoot, and the light in there was that settled light, this burnished thing the April light can sometimes get to be at maybe any o'clock when you are indoors in a low-slung, high-gloss, many-windowed room. Well, I might as well tell you now, the fellow had a little girl there, maybe half the age of our boy. Harelipped—this was the thing—a girl with a bad face to go through life with, and I think I got drunk enough to say to the man, "Aw, God—aw, shit."

THAT'S IT. THE STORY STOPS SHORT right then and there with "Aw, God—aw, shit." Because the next thing you know, it's morning and I am waking up in one of the upstairs beds. But I cannot tell you how I got there. I cannot even tell you what was what between when I was knocking back those Rob Roys and when I was lying down and lifting away the comforter from my head.

There was a carillon across the street. Or across the town. Who knows? It was playing hymns. Or what I think are hymns. As for me, I felt entirely terrific—feeling nothing, not even a tremor, of what you would expect in the way of any aftereffect. What I mean is this—that I had gotten so bad off that I had actually lost time, lost hours—not in this but in real life. Yet there I was, waking up and never sprightlier, never more refurbished in fiber and spirit. Restored, I tell you—I could have said to you, "Look at me, for Christ's sake, look at me—I am in the pink, on a par, up to snuff!" Except for this thing of a whole night having vanished on me—which was something I was not going to let myself think about yet—or which I did not actually really even believe yet—whereas I kept trying to figure out how a thing like this sort of worked, one minute you're on your feet blazing away with a great new friend, the next minute you've skipped over no knowing what, and how did you get to here and to this from there and from that and from whatever that was?

Thing was, I knew I couldn't ask my wife. Christ, are you kidding? But I could smell the bacon down there, and went down, thinking that if I don't get a certain kind of a look from her, then this will mean I must have behaved passably well enough, even if I was actually out like a light behind my eyes. And this is how the whole thing down there turned out, all of them downstairs— host, hostess, wife, our boys—and nobody—wife least of all—seeming to regard me as other than an immoderately late riser and indecorous latecomer to the table.

Coffee is poured, conversation reinstalled.

But here is where the story stops short again. Because—just by way of making an effort to add myself to the civilities—I said, "Wretchedest luck, that bugger, and such a handsome woman, his espoused, the two of them such a damnably attractive couple, and that little girl with the, you know, with the thing, the lip." I mean, I did a speech as an offering, as a show of my harmless presence, the hearty closing up of the morning circle, the one we seek to form to ward off what there had to have been for everyone of night spells.

NOT STOPS SHORT ENOUGH, THOUGH. Because somebody was taking me up on it, converting ceremony to sermon. My wife, of course—her, of course—with that carillon going absolutely nuts behind her. I tell you, whoever it was, and whatever he was playing, the man was good on the thing, the man was getting something colossal from those community bells.

But back to my wife, please—for she nips off a bit of toast and says, "You call it bad luck? Knowing what you know, considering what you know, taking into account all that you know, this is what you say, just bad luck?"

Ah, but this is madness, this is treachery—saying anything about a thing like this when I know it is a thing that ought to be left unsaid. Besides, we had no business being where we were. Even if it had meant keeping to the city and to squabbling over everything in sight, here is where we belong, the city is where we belong, where all the trees worth climbing are kept well out of sight. Those were rich people. My drink, when I was drinking, it had never been anything with the swagger of the armorial in its name.

I mean, what the hell was she getting at, just a harelip?

Listen, I didn't give her the satisfaction. I didn't ask. What I did was go to work on it with my own good sense—trying harder to remember, or to make things up—the result being that on the way home, I came up with a thing that goes roughly like this—the fellow with the little girl sort of producing himself from out of the mist of the rest, me not tracking his features any too clearly, my vision already diminished by at least half.

"Ah, yes," he says, and with his glass he gives my glass a click. He says, "Great to meet the neighbors, don't you say?" He says, "See the fucking neighbors?" He says, "Here's to fucking us."

And me, what did I do?

Say *l'chaim?*

Click his glass back?

"Oh, sure, sure," I hear the fellow say. "Sure, sure—right, right—super, boffo, swell, wouldn't you say?"

I know. We drank.

Did I ever say, "Surgery can handle that"? Is that what I said? Click the hell out of his glass again and say "It's nothing—a good man can fix it right up"?

I mean, what had I said to him to get him to say to me, "Had a little chap of his measure once," and waggle his Rob Roy in salute to my boy? Except all of this, it's all invention, isn't it?—because by then it was too hard for me to tell if we were standing in light or kneeling in water. "Bloody garage door took his fucking head off, don't you know? No, really, old chap. Brand new electric sort of a thing. Electronic, I mean."

We were coming up on a tollbooth, my wife and I.

In real life, that is. But I don't have to tell you I wasn't there with all my wits. "Take this!" my wife was saying, and I took a hand off the wheel to take the coins from her hand, meanwhile still making up sentences to keep filling in for where whiskey had done its best to devise an abyss.

"Nothing against the old homestead, though—no bloody hard feelings."

Is this what I think the man said next? Or something

like, "The fucker drops like a shot the day they finish getting the wiring in."

I don't think I ever got his name, the man who came for cocktails when the neighbors came over and who then took his leave with the others so that the host and hostess could finally sit us down to something—my wife says to cold lamb. She also says she was standing right there and heard every single word, him saying how they'd lost a son but that God had made it up to them with the girl. My wife says the man said to me, "I'd spotted you, you know," and that I said, "For what?" and that the man said, "For a Jew."

But I would not put it past her, making that up, just the way me, I am making this up, especially the part about me hearing the sonofabitch say, "Happy fucking Easter," plus the part about me seeing myself get a hand up out of my pocket to hold his chin in place so that I could aim for right on his lips when that was where I kissed him.

So for what it's worth, that, that's the whole story, and notice, won't you, who just told it cold sober.

HISTORY,
OR THE FOUR PICTURES
OF VLUDKA

HE SAID THAT HE HAD BEEN CONSIDERING the convention of the Polish girl, and I said, "In literature—you mean in literature," and he said, "Yes, of course," how else would he mean? touching eyeglasses, beard, lip while noting that he was feeling himself compelled to take up the pose of the poet in eucharistic recollection of etc., etc., etc.—as literary necessity, that is.

He said, "So can you help, do you think?"

I said, "From memory, you mean."

"That's it," he said. "Any Polish girl you ever had yourself any sort of a thing with."

I can tell you what the trouble with me was—no beard anywhere on me, no eyeglasses either, meat of real consequence to neither of my lips—nothing, at least, to speak of, not enough to give me a good grab of anything, nothing on my face for anyone to hang onto, too little to offer a good grip of me to even myself.

He said, "Whatever comes to mind, I think."

Here was the thing with me—I did not know what to do with my hands.

"Whatever pops into your head," he said, off and at it again, fingering eyeglasses, beard, lip.

The lout was all feelies, I tell you—the lummox was ledges from stem to stern.

"So," he said, "anything you might want to conjure up for me, then? I mean, just the barest sketching, of course, no need for names and, as it were, addresses."

BUT I HAD NEVER HAD ONE. I mean, I hadn't had a Polish girl. What I had had back before this inquiry had come to me was a great wanting to pass myself off as a fellow who had had whatever could be got.

"Vludka," I said, "her name was Vludka."

"Wonderful," he said. He said, "Name's actually Vludka, you say."

"Yes," I said, "and very, for that matter, like it, too."

"I see her," he said. "Stolid Vludka."

"In the extreme," I said. "In manner and in form."

"Yes, the nakedness," he said. "A certain massiveness, I imagine—wide at the waist, for instance, the effect of a body built up in slabs."

I said, "Vludka's, yes. And hard it was, too. Oh, she was tougher and rougher than I was, of course—morally and physically the bigger, better party."

"But smallish here," he said, showing.

I said, "Even said she was sorry about it for the way they were even before she took her clothes off, and then, when she had got them off, saw that what Vludka should have been warning me of was of how big everything else was instead."

He said, "Could tell you'd be lost inside her, awash in stolid Vludka, splinter proposing woodworking time to sawmill and lumberyard."

I said, "Oh, God—cabinetry, marquetry."

He said, "It was impossible."

"I said to her, 'Vludka, this is impossible.'"

He said, "She was too Polish for you, much too Polish."

"So I said to her, 'Do something, Vludka. Manage this for us.'"

He said, "She was pliant, compliant—Polish. You said to her, 'You handle it, Vludka, and I'll watch,' and she did," he said, "didn't she?"

"Because she was pliant," I said. "Compliant," I said. "Polish," I said.

He said, "It took her eleven minutes."

I said, "I sort of knew it would."

He said. "That's how stolid she was."

I said, "It was endless. My arm was exhausted for her. I timed her on my watch. Even for a Polish girl, it was incredible. I tell you, she used a blunt fingertip—even, if you can believe it, a thumb."

"It was ponderous," he said. "Thunderous," he said. "You thinly watching, you meagerly urging. 'For pity's sake—come, Vludka, come!'"

WHAT I DIDN'T TELL HIM is that what I was really watching were the four pictures of Vludka on Vludka's bedroom wall instead.

These are what they were of—of Vludka at the railing of a big wooden-looking boat, of Vludka in a toy runabout with her hands up on the wheel, of Vludka with others on a blanket in a forest, of Vludka squatting on a scooter near a road sign that when Vludka finished doing it to herself she said, "Majdanek, you know what's there? Or was?"

HE SAID, "Well?"

I said, "Well what?"

He said, "What you were thinking—the road sign—Majdanek—what was it that was there?"

I said, "You read my mind."

He said, "No. Just the standard stuff about the camps."

ALL MY LIFE I HAVE NEVER KNOWN what to do with my hands.

Except for shit like this.

THE LESSON
WHICH IS SUFFICIENT UNTO
THE DAY THEREOF

HAVE I NOT BEEN INSISTING it is the most instructive of stories? In fact, it is the most instructive of stories. Indeed, the great thing will be to see if I can uncover the core of the instruction that is prospectively in it. I mean, in the telling, maximize the teaching—do it, and keep on doing it, from the beginning to the end.

As to what I am talking about, it concerns an apple and an apple tree, the one having fallen from the other.

Not that that is all that there is to it. I mean, there are people, there are things. But who has the patience for even the enumeration of these?

Here is the bitter truth.

You have to have the patience of a saint.

Whereas I do not even have the patience of a Lish.

But I should say of a Lishnofski, not of a Lish.

Considering.

Considering the name Lish doesn't point to where I meant to. It doesn't point to the tree I fell from.

LISTEN TO ME talk in metaphor!

Isn't it always the way? One minute, making excuses for yourself—the next minute, making life miserable for everybody else.

It's hopeless.

Let's be honest with each other, I am already exhausted from just this much of it—the story of anything, even the narrating of Gordon Lishnofski.

But there I go again, piling figuration upon figuration. For one thing, Gordon just stands for Morton—and exhaustion, for another, for boredom.

Or nobody calling or coming around to say hi, hello, aren't you swell.

GOD, YOU GET SO FED UP with speech.

Just the idea of telling anybody anything is enough to make you sick, every word weighing tons more than it did the last time you said it—or saw it—or heard it—or wrote it—or thought it. Who's got the energy? Who's got the strength? Isn't this why the apple falls off the tree— from such a heaviness from life, from what's holding it getting weak?

BUT SILENCE IS A TIRESOMENESS, TOO.

This is what my dad's was, wearying all the way. Oh, he was the wordless one, I can tell you. No one came any more wordless than my dad did. But don't think it wasn't a shout to you if you were his son.

You know what his favorite word was?

Atrocious.

Putrid and *vile,* he liked those ones, too.

He'd say, "These string beans are atrocious," and for the whole rest of the meal he would say not one other thing at all.

Or he would say, "These string beans are vile," or

"Putrid, putrid—can you guess what I mean?"

It never occurred to me until right this minute that maybe that this was what they incontestably were. I mean, when I was there at the family table, when did I ever sample any of the vegetables? Who knows, maybe vile and so on, maybe these complaints were restrained complaints insofar as denunciations of my mother's canned vegetables might justifiably have gone.

Considering.

Considering my mother could not actually cook anything any good for you in the can or out of it.

It was just that I didn't care if she couldn't.

Bananas—I loved bananas—and olives and crackers—and licorice—licorice was my idea of great eats as great as they get.

You know how my father would eat an apple? You want to hear how my father would eat an apple? Get a bite off of it and chew it and chew it and then hold under his chin the hand that holds the apple, and spit into it, spit into the hand, spit into it nothing but the chewed-up skin.

I used to think he could do it because of his teeth, or because of his gums, or because of his tongue—or because he had this kind of a cockeyed kind of an articulation and nyalked nyike nyis.

It scared me silly—somebody eating an apple like that, somebody nyalking nyike nyis.

Hey, where did I all of a sudden get all this get-up-and-go from? To speak with such vim and vigor with!

Considering.

Considering that I have been trying so hard to get across to you and to your fruiterer the impression that I absolutely do not give a shit.

So what do you think—fact or fiction, Morton Lishnofski?

I WONDER WHAT it would have felt like, kissing a person with a funny-looking lip. Kissing the person right where the funniest-looking part of his lip is—just imagine it! All I can say is, praise be that in my house we had a host of rules set up to keep the spectre of contagion at a distance, or in check. Wiping off the mouthpiece of the telephone with anything disinfectant—there was one of them for you, and kissing someone on the cheek, there was a second.

I can't think of a third.

Sorry, mind's not quite on enough on what I am saying, I think.

So which was it, Pine-Sol or Breath O'Pine or CN?

I DON'T KNOW ABOUT YOU—but me, I have had enough of this. I mean, how much is it that they can expect a man to take?

Considering, of course.

Considering today's another Father's Day.

Considering that here I am having to sit here and hear myself say all of this.

It's nyile and nyutrid, isn't it?

Or, to get it really hard and right—carbuncular is as carbuncular does—nyanyonyis for atrocious.

Apples falling, falling, falling at all, and then where, where they fall, when they do.

CAN YOU TOP THIS?

LISTEN TO ME, there are a pair of hippopotamuses standing in a river, such a filthy dirty river, it is horrible, it is simply horrible, and the sun, my God, you would not believe it, who could believe it, what with the heat and with the sun and with how sticky and muggy and awful it is, it is stifling, it is absolutely unbelievable how stifling, it is positively beyond all believability, a day so stifling like this day is, a day which could kill you like this day could, a day which could do away with you in just one hour, in just one minute, in just one breath, but meanwhile all day long, from when the sun comes up in the morning to when the sun is going down at night, all day long this pair of hippopotamuses is standing here in the scorching water like this, they are up to their ears, they are up to their eyeballs in the scorching torpid water like this, and it is this filthy dirty hot disgusting dirty scorching torpid water like this, not either one of them moving a single muscle in it, the two of them not budging, not even one inch, not even leaning a fraction of an inch in this direction or in that direction, except for maybe if you want to count these little tiny twitches of the eyelids, these little tiny twitches of the ears, these little tiny trembles you would probably call them, these little tiny trembles and twitches, but otherwise the two hippopotamuses are like granite, like stone, like standing here in the disgusting filthy water from first thing in the morning to the time when

it is almost sundown, all day long the two of them all
covered up by the filthy hot dirty torpid scorching dirty
water like this except for just where their little ears
are sticking up out of it and are constantly twitching
little twitches and for where their big bulgy eyes are
poking up a little bit out of it and the eyelids, the eyelids, you can see the eyelids are giving these little bitty
trembles, these little tiny itty-bitty trembles, these little tiny tremblings like, like maybe from flies probably
or like maybe from little nits like or like from something even tinier than this, or it could be from some
kind of teensy almost invisible itsy-bitsy thing which
likes to creep around on the eyelids of hippopotamuses—but barring this, but barring the twitchings of the
ears and the twitchings of the eyelids, the two hippopotamuses are just standing here and standing here and
you could not even see them even breathing even, because this is how still as stones they're standing, because
this is how still as boulders they are standing, and the
water meanwhile, it just just goes gurgling all around
them like it is some kind of filthy dirty torpid scorchy
syrup probably, or more like it is torpid dirty ooze than
it is like anything like even water even, more like it is
some kind of special water which can get totally
exhausted from just being water, and this is it, this is
how it is, this is how the whole situation of it is from
just after when the sun first comes up in the morning

to almost when the sun is getting good and ready to go down again at night, which is when one of the hippopotamuses, which is when, lo and behold, the hippopotamus which is the slightly older hippopotamus and which is the slightly more overweight hippopotamus, which is when this particular hippopotamus all of a sudden moves his little feet a little teensy tiny bit and more or less just gets them moved into place into a somewhat slightly new position a teensy tiny bit, and then he opens his eyelids all of the way open and he looks all around a little bit and he says, "I don't know—all day long, I still can't get it through my head today is, you know, not Monday but Tuesday."

No, he says, instead the hippopotamus says, "Hey, it's such a crime for me just to stand?"

No, wait a minute, she said he says, she says the hippopotamus says, "Who can think, a thing like this? Can anybody collect his thoughts, a thing like this?"

The truth is this—I don't really remember what the punch line was. But I don't suppose I have the other part much more faithfully recorded, either. You see, I think I was pretty jumpy when I heard it, plus I know I was much too young to be anywhere near old enough for me to listen faithfully enough when big things were probably being said. The only thing I have for all of these years been sure of is that my Aunt Adele hunkered down and told jokes when the cancer started going from her bladder to her bones, that and the fact that my Aunt Adele kept calling up to my house from Miami to New York to tell lots of different jokes to whoever it was who was home. Of course, it was always my mother who always was home—my mother, so far as I can remember, always was. Not that I didn't once pick up the downstairs phone once, and hear something for myself on the order of what you just heard, this plus the power of hearing two women laughing as a child listens in.

THE WIRE

MY WIFE SAYS, "Look at you. Just look at you. How can you look like that? Why don't you take a good look at yourself? Look at me, don't you have any idea of what you look like? What do you think people are going to think when they look at you? Tell me, how can you go around looking like that? Do you know what you look like? You couldn't conceivably know what you look like. Who would believe anyone could look like this? I cannot believe what you look like. It is hard for me to grasp it, a man who can go around looking like what you look like. What is the matter with you, don't you know what you look like? You probably don't have the first idea of what you look like. You act like you are completely oblivious to what you look like. Don't you realize people are looking at you? Have you no conception of the fact that there are people who are looking at you? Why are you so utterly unaware of the fact that you cannot go around looking like whatever you happen to feel like looking like? Take a look at yourself. Just go ahead and just take just one good look at yourself."

This is what my wife says.

As for myself, I used to think it didn't put her in the best of lights for her to be going around being heard looking like somebody saying things like that.

YEARS AGO THERE HAD BEEN a fellow who kept trying to offer me some observations along the very same lines of the ones which my wife, in her time, did. But I didn't see any reason to argue with him, either. So far as his story goes, he's dead as a doornail now, so let's just get his name and address right out here right onto this sheet of paper here—Wortis, S. Bernard Wortis, his conduct of the business of psychiatry being carried out by him at one of the high even numbers on, you know, on East Fifty-seventh Street.

Here's an example of it.

"Just look at yourself. Don't you ever look at yourself? Why don't you come to your senses and sit yourself down and take a good look at yourself?"

But I have always been the sort of person to take a different view of looking.

You take today on the subway, for instance, this woman with this hulkiness of a suitcase . . .

Here is what my mother used to say to me:

"Do you see what you look like? I don't think you see what you look like. How can you let people see you looking like this? You want to go through life seeing yourself looking like this?"

Look, the man committed me and made sure I stayed right where he did it to me to, and this was for just shy of twelve brazen months.

I kept trying to see up inside of her pants past where the crease was.

I'm leaving out everything. I'm leaving out even the

tits and ass of it. I am just too weary of it for me to ever go over the whole history of it in the sense of the whole anything of anything again.

All right, shy of eight months, not shy of twelve months—but since when is time the point?

He said to me, "It's high time you took the time to sit yourself down and take a good decent look at yourself."

Here is what happened on the E train today—the woman the color of what do they say? There is a woman the color of coffee with cream in it, and she's got on short pants on her, and for the top she's got on what I think they call a halter top, and they're both, they are both, the top and the bottom, they have that look, the both of them, that you will sometimes see of their being both at the same time just tight enough and just loose enough, and she has got her hair mown all the way down to her skull to a woolly-looking fuzzy high-domed cuntlike frizzle of a thing—and there her legs are, there her legs are, they are uncovered and glowy right up to almost past her backside almost and crossed in the manner, leg over leg, of how only a woman who gets herself looked at like this ever crosses her legs leg over leg like this—and the eyes and the arms and the mouth and the throat! I mean the things of her, the woman, the things!

She had a small child up on one shoulder.

She was about twenty, and it was—I don't know—maybe it was a baby.

There wasn't any ring on any of her fingers.

The child, the baby, it was out like a light in any light, and I could tell the mother was almost also.

Oh, well, yes—I could see the slenderest of gold ones. Like a wire.

But it wasn't on any of her fingers.

My sister used to say to me: "I don't think you ever stop to think of what you look like."

The building I live in now, hey, it's so full of psychologists and psychiatrists and psychoanalysts and psychotherapists, it isn't even funny.

This whole block is.

They know who Wortis is here.

Or who Wortis was.

His fame went all of the way up from Fifty-seventh Street—or, if the rhyme's all the same to you, came up—because here is where I live up here now.

The suitcase, just to look at it—you could just look at it and tell it weighed a ton.

The first girl I ever tried to get to do it, she did it—but she didn't look like anything, and neither have any of the others of them all of the million times since.

Hundreds.

Thousands.

Not one fucking one!

But what about the girl on the E train today when I was going for the D at Seventh?

Look, you've got a perfect right to know why the man committed me, but tell me something, tell me— can't you already tell for yourself?

I thought: "Someone's dumped her. She's got no one. God has sent me, as my deliverance, this deliverance."

The second girl I ever did it with was probably less good to look at than the first one was. Right then and there, who couldn't have taken one look and doped it all out, the hopeless oblata of desire.

The last one said: "Okay, but do not think you are getting away with fooling me with what you look like, buster, not even for one stinking minute."

I thought: "Wouldn't it be proof of heaven's handi-work if she gets out at Seventh to also change over for the D?"

He said it with the accent on the *nard*.

Dead at forty-three.

Heart.

Heaven was taking a hand in it, all right—except only up to a point it was. Because when she got it to the door, struggling with it and with the baby so pierc-ingly, so pitiably, that it made you want to kill for love, what she said to me was "No" when I said to her "You want for me to come try to help you with it so you can get it down the stairs?"

I'm not telling the whole story.

Tomorrow is June 17th.

That's a little more of the story.

The rest of it is, she said she wasn't going down the stairs, but when I got down them and then looked back up them, then there she was, coming down them and then going right past me on the platform and then going all the way away from me to the end of the platform as far away from me as she could get, all that cargo of her wretchedness notwithstanding.

My wife says, "Who do you think is ever going to look at you looking like this?"

Hey, but guess whose sister the motherfucker was humping when his ticker up and jumped him forty bucks into a one-hundred-dollar hour of friendly family psychotherapy!

Yeah, but lately, lately, what I'd like to know is this: Who has the one validated desperation of my life ever been doing to death for me, *no es verdad?*

MR. AND MRS. NORTH

"YUH, YUH, YUH."

"Oooo. Uuuu. Uuumach."

This is how they wake up. They wake up vomiting. Actually, it is a little after they wake up that Mr. and Mrs. North commence to vomit.

They are not fools.

They know as well as you do the large peril of vomiting in one's sleep. Even in a condition of light sleep, there is the risk of strangulation on some chunk of what gets thrown up from the stomach. The odd bolus of ingestimenta could come skidding back up and lodge itself in some impromptu kink in the food pipe. Even with pillows lifting the head, you're looking for grief if you sleep on your back.

Mr. and Mrs. sleep on their backs. Once abed, this is the posture each pursues throughout the course of the dream-driven night.

They are good sleepers.

They do not vomit until they wake up.

They have separate bathrooms. Mr. and Mrs. use separate bathrooms for the act of vomiting. True, they could both in fact hasten themselves to the nearer bathroom, the one spouse disgorging himself into the sink while the other kneels before the toilet.

Don't ask me why it's not the way they do it.

Perhaps in some families vomiting is a private matter. Or perhaps it is that in this family each of the parties favors the same class of receptacle—Mr. and Mrs. being, after all, husband and wife and therefore alike. Without my speaking of it too descriptively, I take due note that the duration of their relation might have made of them a pair of sink-vomiters or of toilet-vomiters or even of tub-vomiters—vomiters whose practice it would be to vomit into the same style of concavity.

SEE WHAT YOU CAN MAKE OF THIS.

Early in the marriage, mixing bowls were kept at the ready—his on his side, hers on hers—on the floor by their bed. But as the marriage matured, its principals managed to scale certain elevations of self-control—thus making, in the end, the preparation of installing the nearby catch basin superfluous to their needs.

Just as well.

For the bowls were notably unsightly seen squatting there to either side of the bed, where company might spot them when company was taken from the receiving rooms onto a tour of the interior of the Northern family residence.

"What's that?" the alert caller might think to himself—and, getting for his trouble no answer to the unstated but no less tasksome question, presume the offensive and worse.

So the mixing bowls were set aside, and it was a welcome triumph when they were, for now neither Mr.

nor Mrs. has to cope with the nuisance of collecting such clumsy utensils from the kitchen night after cantankerous night. Sad to say, they had, in the old days, now and then quarreled on this score, but only on those occasions when they had both already retired for the evening, having neglected to situate their bowls in place beforehand. First he, then she, or first she, then he, would claim fatigue much too fantastic to undertake the tiring travel all that mileage to the kitchen.

He, for example, would say, "I'm just too spent to do it, my darling," whereupon she would say, "Goes double, my love, for me."

Or sometimes say for me before say my love.

Yet someone clearly had to, and, in the course of things, much as it was contrary to their temperaments, a fearful disputation would ensue until one or the other relented—which one being neither, as a rule, here neither nor there.

Thankfully, the debate over the mixing bowls became, in its time, a thing of the past. What remained to be ironed out was this—who was to have exclusive use of the nearer bathroom? It was vexation itself, this question. Naturally neither Mr. nor Mrs. proved willing to concede that he was any the less in control of his vomitus. To be sure, it seemed unfair that one or the other of them should have to lose one point to win another. So it fell out between them that it was quite properly the Mr.

who ought traipse the greater distance—since this seemed to them the chivalrous, and therefore the more romantical, resolution.

Oh, Mr. North, Mr. North, the fellow insisted he could be happy with this program, and indeed he proved to be—for it pleased him to act in a fashion that promoted his self-esteem, and she, Mrs. North, she, for her part, was happy that her presence created the opportunity for Mr. North to carry out those gestures of courtly conduct consistent with his status as he understood it to rank, a generosity that enhanced *her* self-esteem inasmuch as she, Mrs. North, she, in effect, was providing for his.

BUT AS TO THE PRESENT, so that you might hear for yourself without hearing overmuch from me.

It ordinarily happens that the spouses greet each other before they start to vomit—a hale, a hearty, "Good morning, dearest," or some such expression of politesse. It might even happen that a number of sentences will have passed between the parties before one or the other of them is seized by the first official squeeze of the incipient spasm.

The following passage is drawn from their jointly reported account.

"Good morning, my dear."

"Good morning to you."

"Sleep well, my sweet?"

"Ever so well, thank you. And you?"

"Oh, fine, thank you. Very well indeed."

"That's good. Good . . . good . . . goo-uh. Goo-*uh!*
Uh. *Yuh! Yuh! Yuh!*"

"Uuuu. *Uuuuuch!*"

"Yuh, yuh, ooyuch, *yach!*"

"Uuuuuch. Uuuuuch. Ooooo*wach!*"

And so on and so on, a connubial symphony, an
achievable excellence, the matchless accord of the sea-
soned adventure in the monogamy of the famished.

LAST DESCENT TO EARTH

MUST BE MY THIRD TIME around this time. Or is one supposed to say *round?* Not that I am claiming that this is such a lot, just the three tries, and one of them not even plausibly a try yet, not even decently enough of a try so far that I could quit it right here and still get to count it as anything much more than the start of a start of a try at a try. Great Christ Almighty, there used to be a time when one could slog one's way through twenty, thirty, forty of the kind, knocking one's fnocking brains out over some adverb-ridden thing, proud as punch to have turned one's nose up at as many as that many words. Ah, but Great Christ Almighty all over again, my friends, your parts of speech were no big deal back then.

One had words galore.

One had words to burn.

One had to beat them back with a stick.

I myself had words to kill back then, and did away with as many as the country limit allowed.

Oh, there were sentences to go around back then, and don't let anybody ever tell you any different!

Unless he says *round.*

That I should have said *round.*

That actually it's *round* that would have been the proper way for a proper writer to do it.

MY PAL DENIS SAYS that one of the things which

Nietzsche once said was a thing which went roughly along the lines of a saying like this:

"What good did killing God do if grammar still sasses you back?"

Listen, you think anybody ever needs to be told?

Speaking of which—not of Him or of Denis but just of listening—there is this one fellow who is sitting listening to this other fellow in the two earlier times around when I made the two earlier tries at the story which I am fixing to try to tell you for the third time this time now, just like it right this minute now is supposed to be you sitting, please God, listening to me.

Except they're both, those both, on a plane.

On an airplane.

Which airplane has been going around and around over the airport because the airplane can't get in.

IT IS A QUESTION of congestion.

Or of round and around.

You have to have a runway, you have to have clearance, the traffic is terrific, you think it takes a genius to invent such explanation as this?

Or to tell you how scared to death it is so easy for everyone up in the air for them to get when you have gone from all of the way here to all of the way there but, word to word, the pilot cannot get in?

Save your breath.

Who hasn't himself been through it?

One's belted down into the last seat one's ever going to ever get oneself belted into—while meanwhile the big lunk keeps wallowing the fnock around, no clarification from the fnocking cockpit forthcoming!

So it's no wonder, is it?

That you'll talk just to hear yourself talk?

As one of the men on the plane in the story did.

Or did in the story on the plane.

LIKE THIS:

"Would you believe it if I told you I travel with the dead? No, really, it is actually a business, I am with a firm that operates in this business, for when you sometimes have to have somebody with it if there is a casket which is in transit, either because it is a statute that you have to, either because it is probably a state or federal statute that you have to, or because of the airlines themselves enacting it, a regulation which they themselves have deemed enacted, somebody, a ticketed passssenger, traveling with the dead."

Oh, you could look to me to be talking my head off just as frantically as he is if it was me who was strapped in up there next to the fellow we just sat here and heard—what with nothing by way of a word still to come from the people in charge of the circling and still no hint of the first descent to earth.

But I'm down here writing—and going for my third.

Whereas up there in that, up in that airplane, the man next to the man just listens to him.

Or appears to do.

Not that the fellow talking would anyhow not keep talking because he's so scared.

THIS IS SOME MORE of what, sentence by sentence, the scared man says and says.

"You have to be bondable."

"What if it's really the wheels?"

"You think what they're doing is just killing the fuel for to keep the conflagration only to a minimum?"

HEY, I KNOW HOW the fnocker feels.

They should really have to tell you. Even when it's just routine, I think they should have to keep issuing updates to you and, you know, reassurances, regularly wising you up as to the fact that you are not just going around and around for no roundabout reason at all or, Great Christ Almighty, around when it should be round.

So what's the story?

Go ahead and try for four?

My pal Denis just took off for Ireland, whereas Nietzsche couldn't sit tight, his flight plan couldn't stay put, after Basel.

THE TRAITOR

THEY LOOKED TO ME TO BE TIBETAN or Mongolian or—I don't know, I just want to say it—Burmese. Oh, but this is inexcusable. This is embarrassing. Really, there's not a blessed thing I know about national types like these, about what they're supposed to look like or what you'd call them if you knew. I mean, maybe this couple had actually looked to me mostly like they came from Thailand, but I didn't know how to say it, so I right away gave up on the likelihood because I could see ahead, see the situation of the adjective coming, and knew it would have me stumped frontwards, backwards, sidewards, knew it would have me whipped hands down. Thailander? Thailander can't be right. At least I would not bank on my ever having heard anyone say it—say Thailander. Great day, you'd know it if you'd ever heard anyone say it. But neither can I imagine what you might alternatively say, unless it's Thai*land*ian, which, now that I have actually said it, sounds to me excessively improbable and possibly, to Thailandians, insulting.

You may as well know I once got into some absolutely hopeless trouble over a thing like this—from referring to a certain person by this name rather than by that name. Or it may have been the other way around. Frankly, it was not all that long ago, this misunderstanding. It remains to be proved, in fact, which, if either, was the case—that I misunderstood or was misunderstood. Not that the couple on the subway represented the opportunity for the same sort of confusion. Oh, no, theirs was a confusion of an entirely different sort. I mean, you could see that they were not the kind of people to care a fig for how anyone anywhere might elect to propose a category for them. Or do I mean something simpler and can't say it? But I am a man of action, you see, and not, as you will also see, of words. Although I doubtlessly know more about words than would most persons operating along the lines of the job title I carry with me the Euher and the Thompson to carry out.

Dropped a stitch back there. Had meant to say that these two—that the man and the woman—that what they looked to me like was as if they had reached what is sometimes called "a higher state."

To be absolutely candid with you, I just don't know how I got us into this Thailandian thing. Actually, the more I let thought attack the question, the more I am willing to favor the notion that they, the couple, were very likely Siberian, by which I mean the man and woman who were sitting across from me on the subway last week. Ah, but I forget, I forget—so bundled up against the cold they were, not on your life could they really have been Siberian. Unless, of course, I am making the mistake of believing where you come from has something visibly to do with how you react to what the temperature is where you go to. On the other hand, who is to say one hasn't come to us from Siberian parentage but was nonetheless native to somewhere where one might have grown up warm?

Except they didn't look that way. Not to me, at least. To me, they looked like people who had got used to getting on in measureless abominableness and then had got unused to it. You know what they looked like to me? They looked to me like chumps who were sitting on a subway freezing in New York.

Siberia.

I take it back.

What could I conceivably know about Siberia?

Didn't I say they were sitting right across from me? Because it was actually at a little angle from me that they were sitting—since these were the days when the end of a car on the Lexington line had these two two-seater affairs that were not exactly opposite each other but were sort of, you know, jogged off from each other at a little slant. Anyhow, the picture I'm trying to get painted is it's them on one side and it's me on the other side, whereas as for the rest of the car—believe it or not, because I don't have to tell you, it's not every day it's empty, empty, empty, not one other—hey!—dead soul riding the knife.

Not leastways on this here particular snag of it, ain't it the darnedest?

Well, face it, we tighten it down, it gets tightened down. But can you beat it? From when they get on at

Eighty-sixth Street to when she gets off without him at Forty-second, there is nobody but nobody aboard but I and they aboard.

Or is it them and me?

Now this is the whole point of my telling you all of this in the first place, which is that *they,* the couple, didn't. I mean, get off the train in each other's company. And not only this, but this other *this*—which is that *he,* the Siberian fellow, he tricked her into it—actually faked her out, by hook and by crook gets her off onto the platform and then cuts back into the car without her.

But, damn, with me in it, right?

No, I'm not doing this anywhere near the way I should be. I'm talking and I'm talking—but you do not know what in tarnation that's going on, and couldn't possibly, could you?

I am starting again.

Here is the whole thing from the start of it again.

I said they got on at Eighty-sixth?

No, no, it is I that gets on at Eighty-sixth.

This is my practice—get on where I have to get on— the Lexington line, the Broadway line, here, there, wher- ever they send me, everywhere in the city. But what should instantly give me away to you the morning I am reporting on to you is that it is swept clean of people, the car that I get aboard on—except for them, of course—if they, the couple, were in fact already on it—

the Siberians, the Thailanders, the Mongolians—you
know, the whatever—huddled together in one of the
two-seater affairs down at, or up at, one end of the car—
a man and a woman—this is guesswork, of course—who
I am guessing must be in their seventies at least—just
little disks of faces to guess from, that's how hooded they
are with scarves and caps, these weird foreign-seeming
wrappings. So it is not just the eyes which gives you the
Asian notion, not just the bones around the eyes, but also
the bandaged effect that gets imparted to the head when
these people are looking to get cranked up with some
ceremony or something, or seek protection from the
loosey-goosey elements.

No, that's off.

Does not make any sense, neither.

Oh, Lord, I am really getting out of my depth with
this. It's just you turn on the TV and what do you see
but Tokyo, Seoul, whole columns of them shoulder-to-
shoulder, kids, these legions of kids, brats always up in
fucking arms over this or that, their noggins all done up
with this ad hoc crap on them, the whole street
chuggyjammed with them doing this slow goofy sort of
creepy Bangkokian conga like line.

So this is probably why I almost thought that, actually. Namely, almost thought they might both be Cong
or Jap like, except he was such a tall bugger, six-three, if
I am any judge, whereas as she was a good one, too—the

old woman, I mean—every inch of her as tall as she had to be, and maybe then some on top of it. Not that I ever was standing when either of them was. Not that any of what I am saying to you is anything but a guess. But you couldn't have thought about it anymore than I was thinking about it, even saying to myself, "Make up your mind, guy," meaning I should make up my mind what kind of height I was involved with because I already knew I might have to later on get written some writing about it—a report, at least—and now look, this is just what I am doing, isn't it?—sitting here and getting like debriefed. But so what if she wasn't, and if he wasn't, either? I mean, even if the both of them put together weren't enough to make up even a Maltese dwarf, does this mean it don't count?

Or, okay, doesn't?

IT IS NOT OUT OF THE QUESTION, the truth.

Wasn't there something somewhere in my reading, something I read somewhere where there is this region of the Orient where the people are positively tremendous?

But maybe I didn't read it. Maybe it was in a movie when it was raining and the whole school had to stay inside and couldn't have recess. You know, the climate and the crops and the trade routes of somewhere, setting aside the enormous size of certain of its citizens.

Or maybe we were doing a class project on cotton, and it was also the year of the adjective. Which reminds me to tell you I am not dumb. I promise you, I am more than competent in speaking to the distinction between that which is merely morphologically adjectival and that which is instead, or which is as well, syntactically thus.

Unless you forgot.

I mean, about back there where I was giving the appearance of being flummoxed as to what you transmute Thailand to when you want to say, "I think they both were . . ."

Wait.

When you say, "The man was Mongolian," you replicate the form but not the function exhibited in "The man was a Mongolian."

But I imagine you have gone and forgotten all this. Ah, God, one offers speculations and, once offered, forgets one's own offerings, or speculations. Takes a position and, betaken'd, betrays it.

Man.

My, my—man.

Sorry.

Really.

Been farting around for altogether too long now. You've got me dead to rights—just another two-fisted action type knocking his three-rounder brains out to come across as a powerhouse of thought.

Meant *transform,* not *transmute.*

IT'S SO HARD.

You shouldn't have to know anything to do something. I mean, it doesn't seem fair, does it? But isn't this how the setup is: know-how, smarts, skilled labor?—fellows like me, nothing unwitting, nothing nonpredictable? Ah, it's all such a lousy deal, start off with things which couldn't be simpler, and before you know it, what?

The answer is you're beating your way upstream against great torrents of shit, complexities you never had the gray matter to create. Thought you were just doing arithmetic, yes? Whereas as, Jesus, if you're not Boltzmann, you might as well give up, keep tropical fish, go sign on with the Pentagon instead.

I saw them.

The car was empty.

I tell you, it was the coldest of damnable days! It was New York and there was an icicle up my ass—and them, they—they looked so warm together—they looked like Eskimos together, the dopes, they looked so toughly snuggly with each other, so hardened from, so hardened by, things.

No assumings.

Fact.

Because you realize I am sitting in the seat that is

almost exactly facing theirs? The whole car to choose from, check—but let us not forget the noun to know me by—why I was there then, why I am here now.

You'd look at me and see a fellow who does not look to you like anything—a big man in a big coat.

Lots of room in it for everything.

Oh, you bet, they could have been Aleutians.

They had to be something.

He kept scribbling things. He had in his pocket these folded-up papers and he kept getting them out and scribbling things on them—not words, of course, but numerals, I think, or symbols from applications we keep warning these people they have no effing business messing with. Integrations, disequilibriums—things, didn't I say things? But, all right, this is not my sphere, and wouldn't I be the first to admit it?

On the other hand, just don't think I couldn't see the skunk acting as if he were up to something big—reaching for some elusive result, putting on like some fucking Taiwani or something, like some Taiwanese whizbang, like some trafficker in new methodologies feeling his way heurism by heurism?

You got a beef with it, pal—*heurism?*

Oh, you know, you know—so absorbed he seemed, so thoroughly insulated, so isolated—I don't know—so innoculated from things, the old broad meanwhile nattering away at him, all jabber jabber without letup or surcease—get napkins, get ketchup, aren't we all out of mayo? Or so I was made to make a theorization—because who could fucking hear? And even if I could have, wouldn't it've been in Singaporese?

Or what is it, Singapo?

Oh, yes—Wu, Dr. Wu, this is who is at the bottom of all of this, bigshot sitting over there working out cosmological models in exponents of ten, this Mrs. Wu of his going on at him and on at him, get this, Wen Lung, get that, Wen Lung, him looking at her like he's not listening to the lyrics but only to the tune—all out of eggs, all out of bread, don't forget eggs, bread!

I'll tell you the truth. It wasn't that many minutes between the time I got on and he got her to get off, but it was enough of them for me to make all of this up. You know, Dirac, Besso, Lorentz, and good old Wen Lung Wu, the stinking turncoat humping it on down to the U.N. with whatever he's got going on down there in the language of Hwei.

And doesn't Wennie know it?

Can't old Wennie see?

Can't anybody put two and two together and tell it's three more pages to the end? Hey, who can't figure it that somewhere between here and Forty-second . . . except how do you get out of this, declarative or interrogative? Well, it was all imperative the instant the loose-coated hooligan had got himself all aboard, confederates having cleared away all prior enunciation, confederates having closed off all escape, confederates having screwed down the hatches, having prepared all preparable matters, spot-cleaned the setting for the pointshooter, made way for the ace remover. So what, then, is left for it but for to put the best face on it and for them to huddle in some version of an Asian-ish cuddle? Or vice versa.

Ah, Christ, I hear her say, "Clorox, get Clorox, don't forget, make a note," and him, he writes $OQ^2=t^2x^2-y^2yz^2$ and thinks, "Good-bye, my love—good-bye!"

BUT AS I ALREADY TOLD YOU, the old fraud faked her out at Forty-second. I mean, if he had meant to get rid of her, then this is just what he did—got her off without him, got her good and off and well out of harm's you know.

Oh, the old sly-sides!

I tell you, these people with their eyes, they are not for one minute to be trusted. Why, the rascal, he leapt up with a great start as we drew into the station—fairly leapt, or leaped, I say—as if to say, "Good heavens, Mrs. Wu, your hubby appears to have been incalculably distracted, preoccupied beyond all fathoming—mercy sakes, dear lady, darned near made us miss our station—let us hasten, sweet helpmeet, let us take ourselves away."

Oh, the dickens, the dirty dickens!

But see it as I, your patriot, saw it—the old reprobate

flinging himself at the doors and she, the poor dear, staggering after—so completely bewildered, taken so completely unawares—plunging blindly after, bad on her ancient feet, blisters rupturing I don't doubt, corns, spurs, calluses, great horny bunions—totally but totally disoriented, not to mention so helplessly overcome by such an absolute riot of agonies—but nevertheless making her way just well enough, gaining on her hubby just gainingly enough, while he, the devilish four-flusher, he executes the adroitest of pivots—and all with such gallantry, with the very sheerest of chivalries, as in "Ladies first, ladies first—my very dearest lady of the realm."

Well, you know what I say?

I say he said, "Radies first," okay?

Her safe from me on the platform, him unsafe with me on the train, the whole shebang moving again, hellbent for Thirty-third.

BUT TO BE ABSOLUTELY EVENHANDED, I'll say this for him—which is this—the scamp actually winked at me once the doors had shut her away from me and off we were again, off, off, clattering clangingly along again on our deadly underworld way.

By thunder, the knave, see him sitting back down in the same seat when he lets me have it—nicks his eye at me, like gunfire, just this once—*pow!* Then screws out his folded-up papers, this little stubby nub of a pencil of his, making, for my money, a great Jew-y show of the thing, the filthy fucking Chink.

Oh, let's not beat around the bush, the yig was *Writing Secret Stuff*—isn't it high time everybody quits all this shit and says what he thinks he means?

But here's the thing—which *was* he, doing what he did?—villainous traitor or villainous savior?

Because you can see how it could go either way, answer either claim.

At any rate, it was a local, as I said.

Or if I didn't say it—hadn't!—then I just did.

Forget it.

What we have to deal with is it's next being Thirty-third. This means—go ahead and count them off for yourself—nine to get the Euher out and get the Thompson on, nine to get the Thompson on and shoot once, nine to shoot once and get the Thompson off, nine to do what page 107 is waiting for you to do and then to get everything back in back up back up under your coat.

Which is big for you, and loose.

Adjectives—oh, Christ!

SPELL BEREAVEMENT

MY SISTER SAYS, "It's Daddy. It's about Daddy."

My mother gets on and says, "Don't cry. He will be all right. Please God in heaven, God is taking him into his loving embrace right this very minute and that the man will be all right."

My sister gets back on and says, "Daddy just went a little while ago. Daddy is gone."

My mother gets on and says, "I can't talk. You think I can talk? Don't make me talk."

My sister gets back on and says, "So make up your mind, are you coming or not?"

My mother gets on and says, "No one could begin to tell you. You turn around and the man is gone."

My sister gets on and says, "We have to have your answer. So which is it, are you coming or not?"

My mother gets on and says, "Like that." My mother says, "Just like that." My mother says, "You couldn't believe it." My mother says, "I couldn't believe it." My mother says, "You blink an eye and that's that." My mother says, "Did you hear me, were you listening to me?" My mother says, "You blink an eye and it's good-bye and good luck."

My sister gets back on and says, "Now is when you have to decide. Not next year, not tomorrow, not after we hang up. Do you understand what I am saying to you? I am saying now, make up your mind right this minute now while we are sitting here talking to you because we do not have all day to wait around for you for you to decide."

My mother says, "There wasn't an instant when I didn't expect it, not for years was there a single instant when I didn't expect it. But you think it still didn't come to me as a surprise? I want you to know something—it came to me as a surprise. I can't breathe, that's how much it came to me as a surprise."

My sister gets on and says, "Do you realize we have to make plans? So what are we supposed to do if we don't know how to plan because we don't know if we're supposed to plan for you to come down or not?" My sister says, "Be reasonable for once in your life and tell me do we plan for you to come or do we go ahead and not make plans?"

My mother says, "My head never once touched the pillow when I didn't expect to wake up with the unmentionable staring me right in the face." My mother says, "I want you to hear me say something—all of my life with that man I had to sleep with one eye open." My mother says, "Did you hear me say that? Did you hear what I said?" My mother says, "Please God that God is listening, because I as the man's wife never got a moment's rest."

My sister says, "Make up your mind. Are you making up your mind? Here, speak to Mother, tell Mother. Mother wants to know if your mind is made up."

My mother gets back on and says, "Talk to your sister, I can't talk."

My sister says, "So is it yes or is it no?"

My mother says, "The man was my husband. For going on sixty years next month, the man was my husband. So were you listening to what I said to you, almost sixty years next month?"

My sister says, "Is it the fare? You need us to help you with the fare?"

My mother says, "You don't have the money to come to your own father when he is dead?"

My sister gets on and says, "We have to make arrangements. We have to make calls."

My mother says, "Do you know what it costs to call from Miami to New York? Do you want for me to tell you what it costs for somebody to call from Miami to New York? Do you think they give you free calls when somebody is dead and you are calling from Miami to New York?"

My sister gets on and says, "Look, no one is saying that this isn't just as much of a blow to you as it is to us. But we can't just sit here and wait all day for you to tell us what, if anything, you are going to decide to do. So once and for all, yes or no, you are coming or not?"

My mother gets back on and says, "Let me make one tiny little suggestion very clear to you—where there is a will, there is a way."

My sister says, "Let bygones be bygones—just say yes or just say no and whichever it is you feel you have to say, we give you our absolute assurance that we will do our very best to completely understand."

My mother says, "Talk to your sister. Your sister's listening to you. Try to make sense."

My sister says, "Don't tell me. Tell your mother. Your mother has a right to hear you express yourself as honestly as you can."

My mother says, "Take this, take this—I don't want to touch it—I can't even breathe yet, let alone pick up a telephone and talk."

My sister says, "You're making her sick. I already gave her a pill and now you are making your mother sick." My sister says, "I'm telling you, the woman has taken all she can take." My sister says, "If I could afford it, you know what?" My sister says, "If I had the wherewithal to do it, if I had the money lying around to do it, you know what?" My sister says, "I would run get a doctor for her even if I had to beg, borrow, and steal to do it for her because the woman should be given a good once-over by a good doctor, hopefully a specialist who is absolutely top-notch." My sister says, "But thank God the woman doesn't need it." My sister says, "Thank God the woman has the strength of a horse." My sister says, "God love her, a horse."

My mother says, "All his life the man was not a big

earner, not a big money-maker. But you know something? The man was good."

My sister says, "Let's be sensible. Let's bury the hatchet and work things out together. Do we plan for you to come down or do we not plan for you to come down? Give me a simple yes or no and we will know how to conduct our affairs after we have to hang up."

My mother says, "I am here to tell you, the man never made a fortune, but you cannot say the man was not too good for his own good."

My sister says, "I don't know how the woman is still standing on her feet. Don't torment her with this. Don't you know that you are tormenting her with this? Stop tormenting your mother."

My mother says, "The man was too good. But do they give you a medal for being too good? Listen to what I am telling you, your father was too good. The man was goodness itself. You know what your father was? Your father was too good for this world, this is what your father was."

My sister says, "I want you to know that I am getting ready to wash my hands of this." My sister says, "Are you waiting for me to hang up?" My sister says, "Is this what you are waiting for, are you just sitting there waiting for us to hang up? Because if you want me to get off, believe me, I can get off."

My mother gets back on and says, "The man was a

saint." She says, "Listen to what I said to you, did you hear what I said to you?" My mother says, "Ask any-one—a living saint."

My sister gets back on and says, "No one is saying this is easy for you. Do you think it is easy for me? But things do not get done without plans being made, and things have to get done within no time at all, do you hear?" My sister says, "I have to make certain calls. People have to be called. I am trying to call people and get things taken care of without causing Mother any undue excitement or any additional upset." My sister says, "Consider your mother's health. The woman is not young. The woman is totally devoid of any reserves of energy to draw from should, God forbid, worst come to worst. So don't make worst come to worst. Try to appreciate the fact that the woman is at her wit's end. The woman has not one more shred of energy left over for anymore of your crap. So do I make myself clear? Or do I have to spell this out for you what I am saying to you when I say eighty-eight? Do I have to tell you what your mother has already been through today and she only just an hour ago woke up? So are we going to get your answer or are we going to have to scream ourselves hoarse? Because all your mother wants to know is if she and I are supposed to expect you to come down here or if we are not. So are we or aren't we? Or is it your instruction to us that we are to go ahead and plan your own father's memorial service without his beloved son being in prominent attendance? Is that what your instructions are?"

My mother says, "You don't have to do me any favors. You do not have to do anybody any favors. Do as you please. If you want to come, come—if you don't want to come, don't come—the world will go on very nicely with or without you. Your father does not require your presence if it is too big of a bother for you to come to the man when he really needs for you to be here in attendance here when he's dead."

My sister gets back on and says, "Is he listening to us? Is Mr. Stuck-up listening to us?"

My mother says, "It is not a necessity. There is no necessity. If you can't make it, you can't make it. Not everybody in the world can always be expected to just drop everything and run. I promise you, it is no disrespect if you couldn't make it. No one would accuse you of nothing. Your father would not accuse you of nothing. Your father would be the first person to tell you to do what you have to do if it is a question of prior business making a prior claim on you which couldn't be avoided at any cost. If it's business, don't give it a second thought. So which is it, business or not business? Because if it is business, then it's all well and good. Believe me, your father would be the first one to go along with the fact that not everybody has a situation where they can afford just at the drop of a hat to take time off from their business, come rain or come shine."

My sister says, "If it's the money, then maybe Mother can get you something out of savings and reimburse you when you get down here for whatever you had to lay out for it out of your own pocket. So talk to Mother, tell her what your situation is, tell her what you have in mind, make a clean breast of it with her and get it out on the table with her and I am sure a solution can be found and it will all work out. But if all it is is the ticket down and the ticket back, you could see who maybe has a special on right now for night flights if you left sometime tonight. So why don't you maybe call up around town and get the best price and then call us right back?"

My mother gets back on and says, "The man only wanted the best for his family." My mother says, "The man's every waking thought was for no one but his family." My mother says, "The man could never do enough for his family." My mother says, "The man never wanted one thing for anyone but his family." My mother says, "His family's happiness, this alone is what gave the man life." My mother says, "Wait a minute—not his family's happiness, but your happiness—yours, you, the professor, the poet, his darling, the son."

My sister says, "This has gone on long enough. I am not asking again. Yes or no? Either answer the question or forget about it, because I am hanging up."

My mother says, "It is no crime if you cannot come. No one is going to say that there should be a finger pointed at you if you cannot come. You come or you do not come, you only have to suit yourself."

My sister gets back on and says, "Don't kid yourself, it is a crime, it is a sin, it makes me sick to be his sister."

My mother gets back on and says, "I am just trying to think what would make the most sense for all parties and for all persons concerned."

My sister gets back on and says, "Drop dead. He should do everybody a favor and drop dead. Did you hear what I just said to you? He makes me sick."

My mother gets back on and says, "Be nice. Children, do you hear me? Don't fight."

My sister says, "I am giving you one more chance." My sister says, "Do you want another chance?" My sister says, "As God is my witness, this is your last chance."

My mother says, "He's listening, he's listening." My mother says, "Don't worry, he's listening." My mother says, "Talk turkey to him, tell him what the situation is."

My sister says, "Your mother wants to hear your voice. Try to act like a human being. Is it possible for you to act like a human being? Let the woman hear your voice."

My mother says, "Talk to me, darling. I am listening, darling. Let me hear my darling talk."

My sister says, "Let him go ahead and drop dead. Stop begging him. Stop babying him. Stop pampering him. You know what would serve him right? If he hung up the phone and dropped dead, this would serve him right!"

My mother says to me, "Your father loved you like life itself." My mother says to me, "You know what your mother is saying to you when she says to you that your father loved you like life itself?"

My mother says to me, "Speak to me, sweetheart."

My mother says to me, "Talk to me, sweetheart."

My mother says to me, "Tell your mother what it is which in her darling's heart of hearts."

WHAT IS IN MY HEART of hearts?

There are not people in my heart of hearts.

There are just sentences in my heart of hearts.

So what was I to say to them?

Not to the locutions of discourse.

But to my mother and my sister.

Because I really honestly do not think there was any way for me to say to them why it was I was not answering what they said.

I mean, hey, let's not be ridiculous.

Because you can't just turn around and say to people—good God, not to your own most beloved loved ones—that you are too frantic to talk, that you are too frantic to think, that you are too frantic to pay anyone any attention, lest you fail to have made room in your body for every word as word.

THE PROBLEM OF THE PREFACE

THIS IS A STORY ABOUT A MAN who was done in by a story, and by that, by done in, it is meant killed, done away with, done in, done for—all that. It is a very straightforward affair from its start to its finish, the only question being this—is it, was it, made up? Oh, but no, no, no—the question is not whether this story is made up, but whether that one was, that one being the one our victim was dispatched by, for it was—and here is the nastiest spicule in the whole sorry business—a story he himself was the one who had told.

And had he not?

But tell it he did, and over and over.

As we ourselves shall now have to do, to offer—wouldn't you know it?—the effect of effecting something, lest look inert for having not done so.

Behold.

This is the story the dead fellow was, true or false, both the origin and the context of.

HE SAID JELLY APPLES were coming around and that he hurried to his father to get the money for one and that no sooner did he have the jelly apple and did bite of it then, lo, he set to choking his last upon it, but along came his brother who happened to notice and who got him by the belt and who hiked him up by the belt and who turned him over by the belt and who held him upside-down and who shook him good and proper, such shakings that what had got itself stuck down inside of him came right back up and fell back out of him, such that, by heaven, there our father was, restored to himself and right as any rain and thus a creature who was loving forever everlastingly of his brother.

Never mind this latter's fate.

OR MAYBE HE'D CHANGE his tune and tell it like this—say somebody was coming with jelly apples, so he went and told his father about it and his father said there would always be somebody coming who was going to be coming with something, that if they would not be coming with one thing, then that they were going to be coming with another thing, that there was not anything which they were ever going to be coming with which was not going to cost somebody some money, but that, no, no, the father would not be a father ever to deny any son something, least of all savvy and candied nutrition.

BUT IT ALL WORKED OUT to be the same story, anyway—one bite and the boy was choking to death on whatever he had bitten into—take your pick—sour ball, hot peanut, jelly apple. Whereupon, here comes the brother to come happening along and thereupon to see what lethally gives, so that the brother takes the brother by the belt and yanks the brother up and turns the brother over and holds our father upside-down, et cetera, et cetera, such that whatever it was that had got in him gets knocked loose and comes back up out of him and he is breathing again and is among the living again, even if the whole deal is hokum, hokum, cock-and-bull.

ANYWAY, THIS IS THE STORY the dead man told.

Or *that* was.

But what else could it do but get him killed?

For the storyteller told the story to his children—who just could not wait to grow up enough for them to get strong enough for them to accomplish the same saving feat that had been so robustly extolled of, who just could not wait for them to be ready enough for when their father would start choking enough, which eventually— as it will with any of us—the father regrettably, but not all that excessively, in the event did.

Oh boy oh boy oh boy!

From the children's point of view, it was all for love, whereas from the viewpoint of the father, death was no more than the cost of the narrative endeavor paid out to the end of its aboriginal course. Yet whichever orna- ment you choose to adorn the humbug of the text with, the fact is the kids managed to get the old man head over heels, all right, but then, upended, the rascal slipped loose and cracked something pretty critical, a stiletto of neck bone thence—*oh, shit!*—stabbing its way up into the back of a drastically literal brain.

LEOPARD IN A TEMPLE

LOOK, LET'S MAKE IT SHORT AND SWEET. Who anymore doesn't go crazy from overtures, from fanfares, from
preambles, from preliminaries? So, okay, so here is the
thing—so this is my Kafka story, fine and dandy.
Actually, it is going to be my against-Kafka story. Because
what I notice is you have to have a Kafka story one way
or the other. So this is going to be my Kafka story, only
it is going to be a story which is against Kafka. Which
is different from being a story against Kafka's *stories,*
although I could see myself probably producing a story
against those, too, if I ever went back and took another
look or two at any of the preservations of them.

I'm not interested.

It's exclusively the man himself which I am incom-
petent to be uninterested in.

But not to the extent you would get me to give you
two cents for this person even if he was made of money,
which is what I understand the man in his lifetime was.

I'll tell you about lifetimes.

I have a creature here who is a kindergartner, so right
there this takes care of lifetimes. Whereas I don't have to
tell you what Kafka got was *nafkelehs.*

You say this Kafka knew a lot. But show me where it
says he knew from doily-cutters.

Or even what cutters were who didn't work in paper.

Take my dad, for the most convenient comparison.

The man couldn't make a go of it in business.

In other words, so far as his fortunes went, if dry goods was hot, then he was in wet ones.

But who has the energy for so much history?

Kafka, on the other hand, the louse didn't even know the meaning of the word idle, that's how fast the fellow sat himself down to write his father a letter. But let me ask you something? You want to read to me from the book where it says this letter-writer ever had the gall to ever say as much as even boo to his mother?

Save your breath.

I am not uninformed as to the character of the aforementioned author.

Pay attention—we are talking about a son who could not wait to stab the son of a butcher in the back—but where is it on exhibit that this Kafka shmafka ever had the stomach to split an infinitive in his own language?

Now take me and my mother, to give you two horses of a different color.

You know what?

We neither of us ever had one.

Or even a pony they came and rented you for the itinerant photographer to make a seated portrait.

You see what I am saying to you? Because I am saying to you nothing is out-of-bounds so far as I myself personally in my own mind as a mental thought am concerned—unless it is something which is so dead and buried I have got nothing to gain from unearthing it, which she, the old horseless thing, doesn't happen, as an historical detail, happen to be yet.

But Kafka, so how come wherever you turn, it's Kafka, Kafka?—just because, brushing his teeth, the man could not help himself, even the toothbrush alone could make this genius vomit.

You know what I say?

I say this Kafka had it too good already, a citizen in good standing in the Kingdom of Bohemia, whereas guess who gets to live out his unpony'd life in the United States of unprincely America!

In a mixed building yet.

In yet even an apartment which is also mixed also.

With a kindergartner—who is meanwhile, by the way, looking to me not just like the bug he looked to me like when he came into this world but also more and more like he is turning into a human being who could turn big and normal and dangerous.

You want to hear something?

In kindergarten, they teach reading already. So the teacher makes them make a doily and then lay it down over some Kafka and recite through the holes to her.

This day and age!

These modern times!

Listen, I also had the experience of waking up in my room once, and guess what.

Because the answer is I was still no different.

From head to toe, I had to look at every ordinary inch of what I had taken to bed with me.

Hey, you want to hear something?

I was *un*metamorphosed!

You look like I look, you think you get a Felice? Because the answer is that you do not even get a Phyllis!

Fee-Lee-Chay.

"Oh, Feeleechay, my ancestor is a barbarian, a philistine, a businessman—so lose not a moment, my pretty, if you are for the Virtual, if for the Infinite, then quick, quick, then suck my dick with all swiftiness!

But, to be fair, my mother used to say Klee-Yon-Tell. Still does, I bet.

You know what I bet?

I bet if I ever could get my mother on the telephone, you know what she would say to me? The woman would say to me, "Sweetheart, you should come down here to visit me down here because they cater down here to the finest kleeyontell."

One time I went to call her up once, went to look for her number once, but never did it, never did.

Had to scream bloody murder in my office instead.

Hate to admit it, but I did.

Boy oh boy, was it a scream.

From flipping around the Rolodex cards and then from spotting what was on her card when the flipped-around cards fell open to hers.

You know what I say?

Who wishes the man ill?

But I would nevertheless like to see him wake up to what I wake up to.

Just once.

Forget it.

The rogue was small potatoes.

My dad lived through fifty years as a cutter in girls' coats, whereas Kafka, the sissy could not even shape up and live through his own life.

But why argue?

Where's the percentage?

It wasn't a cockroach on my mother's card.

It was just a very groggy earwig instead.

THE HILT

OH, THE PLEASURE SOLOVEI TOOK in the manner of
Shea's death, never mind that it was a suicide and Shea
the very paradigm of what Solovei could not but help
but helplessly think of whenever he, Solovei, had
thought to set himself the meditation of what it must
be to be the very gentile—oh so very big-boned, so
very large-boned, heavy-boned, long and broad in all
the central categories, the blithe inventor of every
blocky declension, the very thing of this actual life most
actually lived.

And never mind that Solovei loved Shea.

Solovei loved Shea's death more.

Could not keep himself from telling everyone.

"You hear about poor Shea? Poor devil drove himself
off a fucking cliff. Took his car out and went poking up
along the coast and found himself the scenic view that
must have looked to him to be oceanic enough and then
sailed the sonofabitch right off."

Or so the story went.

The story that had been carried cross-country to
Solovei by those who had still been keeping company
with Shea right up until Shea's finale.

Not that Solovei and Shea had ever had a falling out.
Just that Solovei had come to arrive at a time in his life
when it was more and more seeming to him to be necessary for him to keep himself more and more to his
own small experience. This is why when Solovei told

everyone about poor Shea, it was via the telephone that Solovei would pass along the news.

It made him ashamed.

"Hello?"

"Hi, this is Solovei."

"I'm calling about Shea."

"You remember, my old buddy Shea—big guy? Great big happy bastard, great big cheerful happy chap, with this sort of what you might call this indomitably red or reddish or reddish-colored hair?"

"Anyway, I just got this call from the other side of creation and you'll never guess what."

It seemed to Solovei nothing short of a veritable show of heroics in himself that he could keep telephoning the word around when here it kept making the fellow feel so horribly ashamed of himself for him to be doing it.

"Ah, God, the fierceness it must have taken in him for him to have actually taken hold of that goddamn wheel."

And so saying, have a vision of the hands of his friend Shea—great hams of hands, as Solovei understood these gentiles to say in these matters.

Meaty.

Big-freckled.

Letting go and gripping elsewise and then yanking your mind that long, clattering, blazing, disastrous way.

Jesus Christ.

The fucking savagery of Shea!

To which she said, "Oh, it is certainly not a question of living or of dying but only of the hilt."

Solovei did not get this.

He said, "Hilt?"

She said, "Why it has got its teeth so obstinately into you like this, Shea's doing away with himself—the fact that, like his life, how he did it was up to the hilt."

"Oh," Solovei said.

"Yes, of course," Solovei said.

"I see," Solovei said.

"Yes, I suppose so," Solovei said.

And knew his interlocutor had uncovered the truth.

She.

Her.

One of the ones Solovei had stopped feeling the necessity of keeping up with when he had started feeling the necessity of slowing down for himself.

"Come on over and we'll fuck," she said.

"You're spooked," she said.

"It'll get you unspooked," she said.

"Come fuck," she said.

"Maybe sometime soon," Solovei said, and then, with terror in his heart, hung up.

AS FOR WHAT IS LEFT of the story, Solovei never did manage to have his little visit with her but did have, some months thereafterward, a dream in which he had set out to have it, the visit, and in it saw himself in his motor-car motoring along the highway to her house, whereupon suddenly also saw—that is, the Solovei sleeping saw the Solovei driving—suddenly also saw himself having to perform an amazing sequence of unimaginably shrewd maneuvers to elude the enormous truck that had so abruptly been revealed to be bearing down so brutally down upon Solovei from Solovei's blind side, which was both, in his dream, of Solovei's sides.

Solovei could even hear himself already telephoning all of the friends he used to have.

"Hi."

"It's me."

"It's Solovei."

"I was on my way over to see Shea's old wife."

"I had the car out, just to pay a condolence call, and couldn't have conceivably have been driving more cautiously, when out of the blue there is all of a sudden right out of blue this gigantic fucking truck."

"Anyway, it's a miracle, the stunts I could all of a sudden so incredibly do—the steering, the brakes—my reliable, my God, mind."

MY TRUE STORY

MYRNA, LINDA, LILY, JANICE, SHIRLEY, Phoebe, Barbie, Barbara, Sylvia, Marilyn, Elaine, Georgia, Iris, Natalie, Patty, Joyce, Binnie, Velma, Molly, Mrs. Shea, Lucille, Marie, Maria, Valerie, Barbara, Grace, Stephanie, Caroline, Tina, Eliza, Edwina, Evelyn, Edna, Joanna, Jeanne, Janet, Enid, Edith, Laurella, Lorrie, Lorraine, Myra, Emily, Kate, Cathy, Constance, Hedy, Heidi, Barbara, Katrina, Denise, Josephina, Carolyn, Cousin Lettie, Leslie, Lettie, Barbara, Geraldine, Theodora, Patricia, Lena, Lena's sister, Felicia, Emmie, Effie, Ellie, Nettie, Nancy, Blissie, Nell, Nellie, Lilly, Nora, Barbara, Lillian, Helen, Helene, Mrs. Rose, Joy, Ann, Nan, Jan, Deb, Sue, Barbie, Susannah, Suzanne, Mary, Barbara, Barbara, Barbara, Martha, Sheila, Sheilah, Deirdre, Barbara, Cynthia, Cindy, Belle, Betty, Belinda, Bertha, Bettina, Barbie, Betsy, Blossom, Brenda, Brigette, Bronwen, Bessie, Barbara, Barbara, Barbie, Barbara, Barbara.

There have been buckets more than these, of course. But it would be indecent of me for me to list beyond the last name listed. It is sufficient to say I proved to exhibit an exorbitant fondness for the name Barbara and that I finally offered marriage to a person whose name was concludingly thus.

She accepted.

We were wed.

Have lived blissfully ever since.

O, Bliss!

Have been joyful ever since.

O, Joy!
This heart is overflowing.
O, Accepta!
O, Wedda!
O, hoshana in the highest!

HOSHANA?

BALZANO & SON

I EXPECT THAT IT IS NECESSARY for me to tell you the true story of my father's shoes—for I have so often told—if not you, then others—such false stories of my father's shoes, sometimes claiming for my father's shoes some sort of formal irregularity that would enforce the thought of there being a certain abnormality of the feet my father had.

But there was nothing exceptional about my father's feet. My father's feet were perfectly routine feet. My own feet seem to me no different from my father's feet, and my feet—can I not see my feet?—are entirely routine.

Ah, but here I am, already cheating.

I mean, it is shoes, my father's shoes, that I have been inviting you to prepare yourself to hear me tell the truth of, not the feet my father fitted into his shoes.

The firm of Balzano & Son made them, made all of them, dozens of them for each of the four seasons and for all of their uses, all with the maker's mark worked somewhere cunning into the buttery lining of each shoe's interior, Balzano & Son in the left shoe, Balzano & Son in the right shoe, and for each Balzano & Son shoe there would be a bespoke Balzano & Son shoe tree, each rubbed contour a vortical conjugation in wood grain, all formed to fit the exact form of each shoe exactly, this foot, that foot, it too, each shoe tree too, declaring its demand to argue for the theory of its provenance, the name Balzano & Son burnt into each layered grip of each shoe tree, into the grip of the left one and into the grip of the right one, Balzano & Son in the grip of the left one, Balzano & Son in the grip of the right one.

But where is the truth in any of this?

I cannot prove Balzano and his son were not liars.

Who is to say what Balzano's name was before it was Balzano? And the son, what of him? Great Jesus, who's to say the fellow wasn't adopted?

Fellow!

Why fellow?

How fellow?

This Balzano, could not the rascal have elected to change a sex or make an offspring up!

No, I cannot tell you the true story of my father's shoes. I withdraw the statement of my ambition to do so. It was foolish to have boasted of such a project. Such a project is not projectable. Indeed, it may even be that I cannot tell you anything true of anything, save—irrelevantly—to remark that when he succumbed—I mean, of course, my father—I came to have his wristwatch and that it is an Audemars Piguet wristwatch and that it is said to be possessed of such properties as to fetch—appraiser after appraiser so stated to me when I took the object around to them to make my aggrieved inquiries—just shy of $18,000.

Oh, but no again!

I just thought of something.

With respect to my father's shoes, it just this instant occurred to me that there is a little tale I might disclose to you and which could at least have the look of verifiability enough.

This:

That I would take a very good square of flannel to my father's shoe closet to take the dust from the shoes therein, this to show the sign of my devotion to him.

After school and before he came home.

Undoing all of the laces to a depth of three sets of eyelets so as to enhance my labor's not going without the small prospect of being at least a little noticed.

It exhausted me, and exhausted it—the playtime of my childhood—this activity of my youth.

Hours, so many hours.

I suppose.

It does not please me that I lost them.

So do not ask me what time it is.

He is dead and I will be no more nimble.

But will have darkened, and preserved, the name.

THE FRIEND

I LIVE IN A BIG BUILDING and my son lives in a big building, so I meet all kinds and I hear what I hear. And why not, why shouldn't I listen? I am a person with such an interesting life I couldn't afford to be interested in someone else's? They talk, I pay attention—even if when they are all finished I sometimes have to say to myself, "The deaf don't know how good they got it. The deaf, please God they should live and be well, they got no complaint coming."

Take years ago, this particular lady—we are sitting biding our time down there in my boy's place, the room in the basement they got set aside for the convenience of the laundry of tenants.

Some convenience.

Who is a tenant?

I am not a tenant.

This lady is not a tenant.

What is the case here is our *children*, they are the tenants—my boy, her girl—and *theirs* are the things which are in the washing machines and are in the dryers and why it is I and the lady in question are sitting in a terrible dirtiness waiting. So pee ess, it's two total strangers twiddling their thumbs in a room in a basement down underneath a big building, when what you hear from one of these people—not from me, in case you're worrying, but from her, when you hear from this woman I just mentioned a noise like she wants you to think it's her last.

You know.

You have heard.

It is the one which, give us time, we all hear—because who doesn't, just give yourself time, in the long run finally make it?

So I naturally say to the woman, "What? What?"

And the woman says to me, "Do yourself a favor—you don't want to know."

That's it for the preliminaries.

Here is what comes next.

SHE SAYS, "YOU—you got a son—don't worry, I know, I know—and don't think I don't also know what you are going through, either—because I know—I got eyes—I see, I know—so you don't have to tell me anything—you don't have to breathe one word—I am a woman with eyes in my head for me to see for myself, thank you—so no one has to tell me what the score is—believe me, your heartache is your own affair—but so just so you know I know—with him you got plenty, with him you got all anyone should ever have to handle—but I say just go count your lucky blessings anyway—because I got worse—because there is worse in the world than a window dresser for a son—because there is worse in the world than a delicate child—sure, sure, don't tell me, I heard, I heard—and don't think my heart does not go out to you, bad as I got plenty worse of my own—a

daughter, not a son—a daughter—Doris—Deedee—
forty-odd and still all alone in the world—and for why,
for why?—not that someone is claiming the girl is any
Venus de Milo—but so who is, who is?—and is this the
be-all and end-all, to be so gorgeous they all come running?—believe me, she is some catch for the right boy—
for a boy which knows which end is up, this is a girl
which is some terrific catch for such a boy—but shy?—
a shyness like this you could not even fathom—a shyness
like this, who knows how it develops?—even to me, to
the mother herself, it is not fathomable, I can tell you—
so a rash, a rash—like a dryness even, like not like even
a rash but just a dryness, I'm telling you—the skin
here—the cheeks here—so like it is not exactly appetiz-
ing to look at this child at certain periods of the season,
if you know what I am saying to you—but so what is
this?—is this the end of the world, is this the worst trag-
edy I could cite to you, a little dryness the child could
always rub something into and who would notice?—but
skip it—the girl is mortified—the girl is humiliated—the
girl is total mortification not to mention humiliation
itself—because in Deedee's eyes, forget it, this is all there
is, because in the whole wide world there is nothing else
but the child's complexion, the child's skin—so it flakes
a little, so it sheds a little, so for this life should come to
a halt—you don't give them a special invitation, does
anyone notice?—no one notices—who cares?—no one

cares—no one even sees—dry skin, you think people
don't look and see character first?—first, last, and always
what they see is what is a person's worth first—but who
can tell her?—who can reason with her?—it is nothing,
absolutely nothing, the very mildest of conditions—but
for Deedee, forget it—for her it is curtains—that shy, that
bashful, ashamed of her own shadow—so could you get
her to be a little social?—you couldn't get her to budge
for nothing—God forbid someone should have eyes in
his head—a little nothing here—where I am showing
you—makeup would cover it up so who could even
notice?—but does this please her?—nothing pleases
her—her own company pleases her—a movie every
other week, this is for Deedee a big adventure, this is for
my forty-odd daughter the romance in this life—but for
me, if you want to know, from just when for two minutes I think about it, my child alone for all her life, I
could cut my throat for her from ear to ear—forget boy-
friend—does the girl have a friend even?—because the
girl has nothing—the girl has her complexion to look
at—forget a nice decent marriage to a nice decent boy—
and just to add insult to injury, what with so many of
them deciding to be boys like yours is, where even are
the high hopes anymore for a decent healthy girl of
forty-odd anymore?—but meanwhile is it too much to
ask that for my Doris there should be at least a compan-
ion to travel the road of life with?—because, I ask you,

doesn't everybody have a right to somebody?—but her,
she wouldn't even go out looking, God forbid somebody should see a little redness, a little dryness, some
peeling where if she only used a good moisturizer on
herself and did it on a regular basis with some serious
conscientiousness, I promise you, the whole condition
would disappear quicker than you could snap your little
finger—but her—her!—who can talk to her?—my
Deedee—my Doris—God love her—but just thank God
the story at her office it is a different story entirely—just
thank God at her place of business they couldn't get
enough of her—always Doris this and Doris that—I am
telling you, they are devoted to the girl—devoted—
what they wouldn't do for her—like you wouldn't believe it, but just this last Christmas they send her off for
seven days gratis—not one red penny does the girl
have to reach into her own pocket for—the whole
arrangement is already all bought and paid for—the
whole arrangement, to coin an expression, is signed,
sealed, and delivered—and not Atlantic City neither,
mind you, but where but Acapulco—Acapulco!—this is
how indispensable to these people this child of mine
happens to certain individuals to be—all expenses paid,
every red nickel—first class from start to finish—the
best—bar none—so when I hear this, I say to myself,
'God willing, the child will get away, it will be a change
of pace, a nice change of scenery, et cetera, et cetera—

and who knows but that maybe a little romantic inter-
lude for her is just around the corner—after all, a nice
resort, a nice hotel, these Latin fellows, whatever'—but
now I have to laugh—you heard me—laugh!—because
you think Deedee does not come back worse than when
she went?—go think again—this is why I am here where
you see me right now—this is why I have to be here to
do for her and to do for her—the wash, the cleaning, the
shopping, whatever—with my legs, you see these legs?—
twice a week, from Astoria, I have to come in all the way
on my legs from Astoria—but thank God the girl has a
mother who can still wait on her hand and foot—because thanks to Acapulco, look who's got on her hands
a nervous wreck for a daughter—you heard me, a total
bundle of nerves—but utterly—but utterly—say boo to
the child, she jumps from here to there—and you know
what?—I don't blame her—you wouldn't neither—when
you hear what you will hear, believe me, you would not
believe it neither—upstairs up there in her apartment up
there and just sits around all the time listless, no color in
her face, a figment of her former self—would she go
outside for just some air?—goes to the bathroom and
that's it and that's it—who even knows if she goes and
makes her business when I her mother am not here?—
me!—coming in all the way from Astoria—with legs like
these!—if you could believe it, not once but twice a
week—you heard me, twice!"

THE WOMAN GIVES ME on the knee like a tap with her fingers and then she picks herself up and with another groan again she goes and checks on the things she put for her daughter in the machine, whereupon then the woman turns herself around to me and says to me, she says, "Your boy, tell me, are you telling me you got just the one son?"

But why should she wait for an answer?

I promise you, people know there is something which, whenever you look at a father's face, you don't need to ask another question.

"Sure, sure," she says, sticks in two more quarters in her dryer, then comes back to where she was in the first place and plunks herself down in the row of chained-down chairs with another new groan like the last one I forgot the meaning of already.

She says, "Pardon me, but do I still have your undivided attention? Because I know you got your own mind on your own kid and your own troubles, but you didn't hear yet what happened, which is the child goes down there, and it could not be more perfect—the weather, the service, the accommodations—everything is absolutely first-class, so all she has to do is jump into a bathing suit and start being the happiest girl in the whole wide world. But does she go sit around the pool like the other youngsters do so that maybe there might happen to arise a little excitement from whichever

direction? The answer is no—the answer is the girl did
not even begin to give herself credit. Instead, she drags
herself all of the way out to the beach with the wind
and with the sand, which is utterly unnecessary, and
with a book which nobody ever heard of and with not
even a little bag with her with at least a lipstick in it,
not to mention she knocks herself out finding herself
a place for her to sit herself which is as far away from
everybody in humanity as is humanly possible and, lo
and behold, this is how the girl spends the five days, the
six days, whatever you actually get when they give you
one week's free vacation, and not once, when all is said
and done, not once does the girl have a single solitary
conversation with a single solitary human being of any
gender. She reads a book, and this is the entire nature
of her entertainment, period, with the lone sole excep-
tion of this friend she makes, this little animal which
comes running along the beach to her and which
comes up to her, like she thinks like a little Mexican
hairless or whatnot, like this tiny little dog like the
bandleader, if you remember him, used to hide in his
pockets, like a Chihuahua is what they call it, like two
Chihuahuas in his pockets. So the whole first day,
would the thing go away? Forget it, what it loves in this
world is all of a sudden my unmarried daughter. It
could not get enough of my own personal daughter—
huggy-huggy, kissy-kissy, two permanent lovebirds from

the first minute they laid eyes on each other. So naturally the next day the girl can't wait to get back out to
the beach again, God forbid her friend should miss her
for two minutes, and this time she's got with her what?
Because the answer is a handbag. Do you hear this, a
handbag! But for lipstick and mascara and eye shadow?
Don't make me laugh. Because the answer is it is not
for something serious but instead for the child to sneak
her brand-new one-and-only in through the lobby and
up in the elevator and for the rest of the whole vacation feed it scraps from the table and watch it sleep
between two clean sheets in the bed with her like a
person, please God it should not all night long have its
little head on its own personal pillow. And why not? In
all of the girl's whole life, aside from her mother, who
ever paid her two minutes of attention before? But on
the other hand, outside of her mother, tell me who ever
got the chance! Even the girl's own father, may the man
rest in peace, he had to hire an army every time he
wanted the child to hold still so he could talk to her
or get even in the light of day even a good look at her.

"SO NEXT COMES THE TERRIBLE CRISIS.

   "Are you listening?

   "Because time's up and now you have to gather yourself together and pack your luggage and face the facts
that you threw away your one big chance and say so

long to paradise. But could the girl even begin to tear
herself away from the first real friend she ever in all her
born days ever had? This thing, could the child just say to
it this is it and this is it, now good-bye and good luck?

"Don't hold your breath.

"Weeks later, when she could first open up her mouth
to even first begin to speak again, the child actually said
to me, 'Mother, I think I would have eaten poison before
I could have left it behind. *Poison!*'

"Poison, some joke.

"Believe me, when you hear what's coming, you will
say to yourself the same as me, ha ha, poison, this is a
good one, this is some joke, poison.

"So don't ask me why, but this is how determined the
girl is, because even with all of the reasons nobody in a
million years could get away with it, the answer is she
did. All the way back to New York, right past all of the
big shots with all of their badges and everything, and
then right out of the airport past the customs and the
rest of it, and then right back here into this same building right here where, God love him, I know, I know, your
child has got his own problems too, your own lifelong
heartache has got his problems too, what with all of his
gorgeous costumes and with his window dressing and
who also rents a nice dwelling in the building—from
Acapulco to New York, here comes my Deedee, my
Deedee, with her beloved!

THE FRIEND · 163

"But as soon as it gets here, would it eat? Could she get it to do anything but drink water? Maybe the airplane ride gave it an upset stomach, who knows?—meanwhile all it wants is water and to lay around and vomit, and it wouldn't even touch a single morsel or have the strength to play with her or even let her kiss it. So by now the girl is thoroughly beside herself with panic—she is so frantic the child cannot even see straight—so what does she do but pick the thing up and wrap it up in a towel because it is cold out and God forbid her adorable darling should catch a chill and get any worse off than it already is—and like a maniac she runs out into the street with it—like a crazy woman she runs to go find the dog-and-cat doctor which is up the block from here after you pass the big Shopwell in the middle of the block.

"God bless him, the man can see with his own two eyes the girl is positively hysterical—so he quick puts everything to one side and takes her right in, says to her, 'Sit, wait,' he'll be right back with his diagnosis, first he's got to get out his instruments, first he's got to examine, the child meanwhile shrieking, 'Don't hurt him, please don't hurt him!'"

The woman looks at me and she says to me, "So did you hear me with both ears—instruments, examine—don't hurt him, please don't hurt him, please?"

She gives her chest a grab like there is gas inside of it, and she says to me, "Go check your machine—there's time yet—because with problems like ours, who are we kidding, where do we think we are running?"

YOU THINK I DON'T KNOW a storyteller like this one? I promise you, I myself in this department was not exactly born yesterday, these people with their teasings, with their winks, with their punch lines. But by the same token, who wanted to offend such a person? Because, for one thing, you never know when you might require the company, and meanwhile let us not forget who else of my acquaintanceship also makes his residence in the very building and could always use a friendly neighbor's mother with an open-minded opinion. So this I can give you every assurance of, I myself did not intend to go burn up any bridges behind me.

This is why I got up and felt inside of the dryer— even though I did not even have to actually touch anything to see that they all had for them a little way still to go yet. And then, like a perfect gentleman, I come back and I sit down and I signify to the woman I am all ears and at her beck and call whenever she is ready to please continue. But strictly between you and me, so far as punch lines go, in all of history they still never invented a second one.

She says, "Two seconds."

She says, "The man is inside of there all of two seconds with his instruments and his examining."

She says, "The man comes out with his white coat and with his rubber gloves and he says to the child, he says, 'Darling, I am afraid I must inform you your pet has a mild case of rabies—you didn't get near any of its saliva, did you?'

"'Oh, God, God!' my daughter screams, and then it dawns on my Deedee, rabies, and she shrieks, 'No, I'm fine, I'm fine—just give me back my dog, I want to get a second opinion, I want to see another doctor!'

"So what does this one say to that?

"Mister, are you listening to me when I ask you what this one says to that? Because here is the answer the whole wide world has been waiting for. Which is that this man, this doctor, this specialist, he gives the girl a look and he says to her very calmly to her, he says, '*Dog?* That animal in there is no *dog,* lady. That animal which you brought in here is a *rat.*'"

YOU KNOW SOMETHING?

Because I am telling you the truth when this is what I sit here and tell you.

For some crazy reason, after I hear what I hear, I do not know what the next thing for me to do is. I mean, my son's clothes—I do not know if I can bear to touch them anymore—not even when I know that if I go to get them, they would be as clean and as dry as a bone.

AGONY

IN THAT CASE, THERE WERE two men and a woman. The photographer may also have been a woman, for there to be someone to go with one of the men. But I never looked to see. I only looked to notice the others— which is to say the three persons who were readying themselves for the photograph and who, accordingly, kept their backs turned to me.

Perhaps their span hid the fourth party—which is to say, the party with the camera.

Which is to say, why did I not notice the photographer, since the persons getting themselves ready for the photograph faced away from me and, therefore, I must have faced the fourth party?

I cannot say what the three of them looked like, since I only saw them from the back—except that the men were husky by my standard, wide-waisted, one man considerably the taller of the two. And there was this: the woman had no appeal that I could see.

My attention was mainly elsewhere. It was captured by the placement of the arms of these people as they prepared themselves for the photograph, the woman between the men, the men reaching back behind the woman to rest a hand on each other's shoulder, the woman with both arms reached out behind the men, to hold each man from behind, her fingers taking the man tight by the waist—wide waists, as I remember it, in each case, the men's waists.

They all hugged like this when they were ready.

Then they dropped their arms, and you knew, without needing to be notified, that the photograph had been completed, or don't you say taken?

I kept standing there, to see them stand there for a while, facing away from me, all three, the two men and the woman, their arms at their sides—each of the three of them with arms no longer in the exertion of a pose.

I remember something else now.

One of the men—the shorter, I think—wore very bright corduroy trousers, a very bright green, I would say, and a very pale yellow sweater.

Ah, but then they had their arms reached back up into place again. Or places, do you say?

They were getting themselves in readiness again.

They hugged.

I could tell they were hugging hard.

Then they let their arms fall to their sides again, or is this to say that each person lowered his arms swiftly to his sides?

You could anyway see another photograph had been made—or taken—and that this was to be the last of the photograph-making or photograph-taking.

MY SON WAS IN MY COMPANY for the day.

It was to be a day for us in the park.

He was riding his bicycle and I was with him to see him

do it. But for the time I was noticing the photograph-taking, I was not seeing my son ride.

But when I resumed doing what I had been doing, I saw he was riding very well—and even doing some tricks. Or if you say acrobatics, then that.

I called to him.

I said, "Come over here a minute!" He rode up to me.

He said, "How did you like it?"

I said, "I've got a good idea."

He said, "Did you like the way I did it?"

I said, "Let's go home and get the camera and then we'll come back here and we'll take a picture of you with your bike."

He said, "What do you think of what I did?"

I said, "Let's go home. Let's get the camera."

WE DID IT.

Which is to say, my son and I went home. But we never got the camera for us to go make a photograph of him in the park with his bike.

Something came up.

I don't remember what.

But something did.

My plan was to produce a photograph.

My plan is to have the camera with me the next time we go. My plan is to find somebody and show him how the camera works.

My plan is to hand over the camera and then take my place behind my son.

The way I see it, the bicycle will be positioned broadside to the camera, my son situated on the seat, in an attitude of motion and of happiness perhaps. I will be standing just rearward of him, my arm arranged across the shoulders, this or some other such gesture to indicate that I am touching him and am keeping him, will always keep him, from falling over.

And then we will be like this.

DON'T DIE

MY FACTS ARE NOT UNKNOWN. This notwithstanding, mine is a history which has never been without its share of detractors. But I feel, however, that we can safely say the truth must speak for itself. For example, the period of incarceration was not excessive. As an institution, it was viewed in the highest regard. Each and every member of the staff was of a generously professional caliber. I am not claiming to the contrary, or asserting in any fashion, that there might not have been the infrequent individual incorporated here and there who would not in every respect pass muster under the harsh light of what we so fondly refer to in our thoughts as our contemporary nationalistic standards. But it goes without saying, this notwithstanding, that you cannot judge yesterday's failure by today's success. To postulate the direct negation of this would be to go too far and to currently commit a travesty against the race of mankind and, of course, speech itself, splitting, or cleaving, the complaisant infinitive. Yet speak one must, and this quite obviously means me. My statement is this—more dereliction would be more than welcome. At that time, and since, even I, at my utmost, was not privy to enough information. Therefore, I can, as is understood, speak only without the benefit of diametric contradiction, unless more is expected of me, in which event I would not be adverse to holding myself, and the other panelists in my party, in substantial abeyance, both now and otherwise.

Little, or even less, will it profit us, I think, nor the generation to come after us and to cross-index us, to offer up for ourselves various personal and sundry opinions disproportionately or needlessly. Trust, we can agree, is paramount, now as never before. It is on this account, and only on this account, that knowledge of the facilities must be tolerated if not lauded. Persons to have come before my ken, which, admittedly, is and was the limited ken of the patient, deserved every consideration as one professional to another. Nevertheless, although I was not mental in my mind, nor even under suspicion by those responsible for oversight, I was cared for. My debt is great. I would mention the name, but there are legal reasons. Suffice it to say, due reference has been made in the writings of others as well as can be expected by us as well as by our detractors, both preponderantly and paradoxically. The answer is inescapable, not only for the time being, but also for the good of the community. May God protect us. We can do no more nor do no less. Meekly, mildly, and with consciousness aforethought, neither I nor my family bears them any ill will. Speaking in summation, then, as one who has spoken the truth, let us turn our attention to Nurse Jones.

Now, if we were to turn our attention to Nurse Jones. Now, if you will turn your attention to Nurse Jones. (A cognomen surely.)

WHAT MY MOTHER'S FATHER WAS
REALLY THE FATHER OF

THESE ARE THE THINGS she said to me.

MY MOTHER SAID HER FATHER was as strong as a horse—she said her father was as big as a horse, and also as strong as one, too.

MY MOTHER SAID HER FATHER was a giant of a man, that he was a regular six-footer, that people were always shouting up at him to try to get him to look down at them and maybe to be their friend. She said people were always shouting, "Hey, Mister Six-Footer, tell us what the weather is like up there? Is it already raining? Is it or isn't it snowing?"

MY MOTHER SAID TOTAL STRANGERS could not get over it, the tallness and the strongness of the man. My mother said complete strangers were always passing comment on it. My mother said, "Not like with some people I could name." My mother said, "With some people I could name, they go into a room, no one gives them the first courtesy of even taking any notice. You would not, with some people I could name, not even take any notice such people were in the room at all."

MY MOTHER SAID, "Stand up. Look like you are somebody. Try to look like you are trying to amount to something. Show them who you are. Make believe you are

who you say you are. Are you putting your best foot forward? Put your best foot forward. Show them you intend
to be a member of the human race. My father was a
member of the human race. My father was not like some
people I could name—not big, not strong, not even a
member of even themselves."

MY MOTHER SAID ANYONE could look and see that
her father was a person of unquestionable refinement.
She said, "You don't have to take my word for it." She
said, "Ask anyone." She said, "Why should I all by myself have to be the whole judge and jury?" She said,
"Why stand on ceremony?" She said, "You can go ahead
and satisfy your curiosity any time you want." She said,
"I can wait. I've got the patience. I've got more than
enough patience for the both of us." She said, "Believe
me, I've got enough patience for the whole country of
China, not to mention his brother Siam."

SHE SAID, "YOU NAME THE LANGUAGE, my father
could talk it." She said, "Where was the man's nose?" She
said, "The answer is forever in a book." She said, "There
was no telling what the man might have made of himself if God had only given him a decent interval to do
it in."

MY MOTHER SAID HER FATHER was the Father of the

Steam Engine and the Father of the Refrigerator and the Father of Certain Other Creations, but that the stinking gentiles came in and took advantage of the man's good nature and stole all of the man's blueprints from him, so that now you would not find the proof of it not anywhere in the world, not nowhere on earth was there one stinking way for you to get the proof of all of the things which my mother's father was really the father of, capital F, mind you, capital F.

YOU KNOW WHAT MY MOTHER SAID? My mother said with just his little finger he could have broken every bone in all of their whole stinking rotten gentile bodies, but that the man was too refined of a person for him to lower himself down to their dirty stinking rotten level where somebody might catch him stooping to do it.

SHE SAID IT BROKE her father's heart, the dirty stinking way they all stole from him, the gentiles and the government and the landlords. She said, "But you know what?" She said, "The man would not retaliate. The man would not retaliate against them for one filthy dirty stinking rotten lousy single instant."

MY MOTHER SAID, "Listen to me, I am here to tell you, the man was a saint, and this is what it was which killed him, saintliness, pure and simple."

SHE SAID, "TAKE ONE GUESS who you remind me of." She said, "Because he, him, this is who, ask anybody, you remind me of."

SHE SAID, "YOU KNOW what you are?" She said, "You are too decent, you are too good, you are too sweet-natured. That's what you are."

SHE SAID, "I AM GOING to tell you the truth—you are too good for your own good."

MY MOTHER SAID, "A creature like you, how could it expect to fend for itself?" She said, "A person has to be a bully, a roughneck, a hoodlum, a criminal."

SHE SAID, "I KNOW YOU, I'm no fool—wild horses could not make you get down with them on their dirty stinking rotten level—the gentiles and the government and the landlords."

SHE SAID, "Throwbacks, this is what I call them." She said, "I call them throwbacks—and you know what else?" She said, "I am not ashamed to say so to their face!"

SHE SAID, "DON'T THINK I don't know." She said, "I know." She said, "I promise you, I could give the whole stinking gang of them lessons!"

SHE SAID, "YOU WANT TO HEAR something?" She said, "Sit yourself down for two seconds and I will tell you something." She said, "I had to be made of iron." She said, "This is what I had to be made of—of iron!"

WHEN MY MOTHER GOT OLD and sick, she said that when she was a little girl in an orphanage, that they gave out bread and jam in the orphanage, that they gave it out every day at three o'clock in the orphanage, and that she always ate hers the instant they had given it out to her, but that her big sister Helen didn't, that her big sister Helen saved the bread and jam that they had given out to her, and that her big sister Helen always put her share away somewhere for later, but that later, that when it was later and when my mother got too hungry for her to wait for supper anymore, that her big sister Helen would go get the bread and jam she had been saving for later and that every day she did this, that every day my mother's big sister Helen would have saved her bread and jam for herself but that she would come running with it for her to give it to my mother.

WHEN MY MOTHER GOT OLDER and sicker, she said that sometimes the streetcar would come banging up the hill at the same time the clock was banging three o'clock, and that she thought that if you could hear both of them going outside and inside at once, the streetcar in the street and the clock in the orphanage, that then it was a secret sign to you that said that you were going to get a visit, that said to you getting off of the street-car here comes one or the other of them, that getting off the streetcar your mother or your father was coming to you, but that there never, not once, was either one of them coming to her, not either her mother or her father. And that then when it wasn't, that then she remembered her mother was crazy and her father was dead.

MY MOTHER SAID, "This was why I had to have my big sister's bread and jam—because my mother was crazy and my father was dead."

MY MOTHER SAID, "Mine wasn't ever any good any-more because of being eaten and cried on it."

LISTEN TO ME—you know what my mother once told me when she thought she was going to pass away?

MY MOTHER SAID her big sister wasn't really the one who was the older one—this and that their father, that the man just went away.

SO MUCH for your brother Siam.

THE DOG

I WAS NEVER IN A PLACE LIKE THAT. I was an American boy when they had places like that. So everything I say is just me imagining things. Except for the names, of course. I know the names. I have a list. I have been making a list. You couldn't guess the names I already have on it. But I am not anywhere near finished yet. There is just no telling what it is going to take for me to get the list completed. Because the point of this is they only want you to hear about a handful. They only want you to hear about the same ones which they want you to hear about, which are the same ones which everybody all over the world has already heard about. Whereas there were secret ones. There were hundreds of secret ones. Even hundreds is a big understatement. Not even thousands is an exaggeration. You think thousands is an exaggeration? Because it's not! Because they had them everywhere. You couldn't guess where they had them. You would faint dead away if I told you where they had plenty of them. You would think what a liar I was if I told you, or was crazy or was worse.

Here is one of the famous ones.

Ravensbrück.

You probably heard of that one.

Did you hear of that one?

I just told you—so now you heard of that one.

Not like Oswiecim.

Imagine having to say Oswiecim morning, noon, and

night. This is probably why they didn't call it Oswiecim but called it Auschwitz, even though, hey, Auschwitz wasn't its real name.

But take my real name.

You know what I should do?

I should probably have a list for it.

WHAT IF THEY HAD A BARBER at Treblinka?

Or at Buchenwald?

Or at Dachau?

I have been thinking about this. I have been thinking about what if they had to have a barber to get off all of the hair off of them for when the women came in and the girls—get off all of their hair off everywhere— because didn't they do that, didn't they take off their hair off for something, didn't they take it all off of the girls off and the women for some us-hating purpose?

So they must have had a person who did it. They must have had a person who cut off the hair off. It must have been a person who would be good at it and who would not get tired from doing it and who would know how to keep on doing it, to keep just cutting and cutting and not giving anybody who asked the wrong answers. Because look at how hard it would be for you to just keep doing it, you would have to be a one-hundred-percent professional—all of the girls coming in at you and taking their clothes off and all of the women.

So what do you think about the question of who would be the person who did it?

You think it would be a job which they would give to what kind of a person?

Tell me which sex at least!

Tell me how old in years at least!

Tell me if this person should be a person who is short or who is tall, just as far as someone reaching!

BETWEEN 1938 AND 1944, I made regular visits in from Long Island to my father's place of business. It wasn't just my father's business. It was his business in business with his brothers. It was the business of making hats for girls and for women and then of getting places like Macy's and Gimbel's to buy them and make my father and his brothers rich. So I was telling you about between 1938 and 1944. Because I would come visit my father at my father's place of business and my father would show me around to all of his workers in all of the divisions and then my father would call up for his barber to come up for him to give me a haircut, and then a man would come up and would do it.

Then this is what my father would say.

"Now that they've cleaned you up, let's go out and put on the dog."

Then my father would give the man the money and

take me out to a Longchamps for lunch and then, later on, take me over to DePinna's for something new, like for new leggings or for knickers to go with my new coat.

The money my father gave the barber, you know how he did it, gave him the money?

He slipped it to him.

My father slipped it to him.

You know, slipped it, palmed it, passed it off—a way the handler works the hand.

BIRKENAU.

Carthage.

Oz.

New York.

KNOWLEDGE

SHE SAID, "YOU WANT ME TO KISS IT and make it well? Come sit and I will kiss it and make it well. Come let me see it and I will kiss it and make it well. Just take your hand away from it and let me just look at it. I promise you, I am just going to look at it. Oh, grow up, could looking at it make it worse? Do us both a favor and let me look. I swear, all I am going to do is to look. So is this it? Are you telling me this is it? This can't be it. Are you sure this is it? You are not really telling me this is what all of this fuss is about. Is this what all of this fuss is about? I cannot believe that this is what all of this fuss is about. You have been making such a fuss about this? Don't tell me this is what you have been making all of this fuss about. You call this something? This is not something. This is nothing. You know what this is? I want to tell you what this is. This is nothing. Does it hurt? It doesn't hurt. It couldn't hurt. Why do you say it hurts? How could you say it hurts? You really want me to believe it hurts? Is this what you are telling me, you are telling me it hurts? Because I cannot believe that this is what you are telling me, that you are really telling me that a thing like this could possibly hurt. A little thing like this could not possibly hurt. Do us both a favor and don't tell me it hurts. So when I do this, does it hurt? What makes you say it hurts? Are you certain it hurts? How could it hurt? Give me one good reason why it should hurt. I should show you something that hurts. I am going to give you some advice. You want some advice? Count your lucky stars you don't have something that hurts. You know what you are doing? Let me tell you what you are doing. I want you to sit here and hear me tell you exactly what you are doing. Because guess what. You are making something out of nothing. You want me to tell you what you are doing? Because this is what you are doing—you are making something out of nothing. So don't act like you didn't know. You know what? You're not doing yourself any good when you put on an act like as if you didn't know. I am amazed at you, always putting on an act. So how come you never figured this out for yourself? You should have figured this out for yourself. Why should you, of all persons, not be the one to figure this out for yourself? I want you to promise me something—next time promise me you will figure things out for yourself.

Forget it.

I do not need anybody to promise me anything.

Let me ask you something.

No, better not, better skip it.

The answer would make me sick.

Listen, you know what is wrong with you? Because there is something very, very, very, very, very, very wrong with you. I guarantee you, I promise you—a person's mother, a mother knows.

BEHOLD THE INCREDIBLE
REVENGE OF THE SHIFTED P.O.V.

HOW SHALL WE SAY THE CLOCK WAS BOUGHT and paid for? For surely the seller's sticker on the thing declared a figure remarkably bolder than these youngsters could decently manage. But they were so keen, the two of them, so ungovernable in their zeal. Of what earthly pertinence was it that their purse could scarce stand up to the swollen demands of the humblest item in this shop? And the clock, oh my, as to its forbidding tariff, great heavens, this, please be clear, was certain to be seen by most shoppers as another, and much harsher, matter entirely. But what, please be, did other matters, certain or otherwise, have to do with anything when it was naught but the pressure of necessity itself that rested its infinite weight on the possessed hearts of these young people? For there the clock stood in its stony oaken case, all solemnity in its olden bearing (after all, the sticker stated "Early Nineteenth Century" no less legislatively than it stated the price) as it spoke its artful speech of sturdiness, of continuity, of permanence, offering to deliver these affiliations first and therefore, when the time was right, everything else.

It said it could confer on them as much.

Or so we heard it pledge its word to the new home-makers—and they heard it too.

"Wow, that's no joke!" the boy announced with some excessive gusto, meaning to exaggerate his astonishment not just for the good fun of making fun of himself but also to suggest to the shop's proprietor—who had hovered into position—that, in fact, for these two customers, the amount would be no large sum at all.

"But only think of it!" the girl exclaimed. "I mean, wouldn't it be like an heirloom really? I mean, when we have a family, couldn't we just sort of pass it on to them the way real people do, sort of like generations upon generations forever?"

The boy colored at his spouse's high sentence, wanting to hurry to correct her where it had struck his ear that the girl had gone with it, great Christ, a measure or two too far. But the boy knew the damage had been done, that it was always already centuries too late ever to withdraw the smallest wrongness, that the proprietor— the man hovering ever more tellingly into position—a lofty enough presence to hover, actually—had heard all, judged all—"generations upon generations forever" indeed!—doubtlessly savoring the evidence on a tongue that would publish conclusions elsewhere.

Ah, God, the boy could hear the verdict carrying down the ages after him: "Innocent young dear has gone and got itself a goodish burden, now hasn't it? Dreadful silly luckless sap."

That did it, or so it seems not unsafe for us, less lucklessly, to suppose.

At any rate, grinning horribly, the boy motioned for the girl to fetch the "family" checkbook from her handbag—so that, by whatever means fiscal, the clock was got—and a note was accordingly made and thereafter wired to the fancy key that poked from the fancy keyhole whose lock could let you get at the lordly pendulum either for the business of starting it up or, if ever required, shutting it down.

Sold.

And so forth and so on.

We are reporting they bought the clock.

A "GRANDMOTHER CLOCK" was what status the thing was rendered by the reference books in which its kind was pictured, this, it is not unlikely, in pursuit of a program to restrict the object to a rank not so grand at all—and though the provenance of the clock was very probably more local than not, still (the seller had seemed so tall, so hovering, so . . . *otherly),* once the clock had taken up its post against their bedroom wall (there was really nowhere else for them to fit their purchase, what with the premises being—the marriage was hardly yet out of its cradle—so cruelly unbaronial), the owners succumbed to the practice of engaging the phrase "our imported piece" whenever inquiries were made by one or another young couple who, after very persuasive fare indeed, at the card table set up for the purpose in the kitchen, were escorted back into the bedroom for a bit of TV with coffee, dessert, and cordials.

"Oh, but it's so unutterably special," the other wife would say. "No wonder you want it back here where you sleep, where a chic antique of its type can really be better appreciated on a much more frequent basis."

"Yeah, nice," the other husband would say. "So you guys inherit it from your families or something?"

But whatever enthusiasms the other young couple would insert into the ethers as they bit into cake and drank from goblets and sipped from demi-tasse cups no bigger than big thimbles, sooner or later someone would be bound to observe—generally when the clock's imperturbable chimes were finally being heard from—that the time was the better part of an hour fast.

Or slow.

But wrong.

Fast or slow but wrong.

Always wrong.

Never not anything but chaotically wrong.

Off.

Way off.

Not right.

Not once.

Nope, nowhere even close.

THERE WAS NO REMEDY for it.

Years into the marriage, the thing still tolled the hour nowhere near the hour—and when one went to the living room (oh, as they will to all couples who achieve the early stewardship of a magisterial object, other important possessions had issued to our couple, even a commodious enough living room had) to see what time it was, one had to smack one's head and reinstruct oneself that for such a use, for telling the time, the clock was no good at all. Whereupon, whichever of them it was, this party would then get himself prayerfully down onto his knees, would work the fancy key, would draw open the panel whose business it was to keep from view the relentless commerce of the pendulum, would put a finger out to stop it, would then reset the whole affair, hideously mindful all the while that whatever adjustment was being made will have long since, hours hence, begun to yield to the mischief transferring exacting correction into more and more violent error.

The bother was pointless.

Clock people were summoned from other counties, from distant precincts, from bizarre neighborhoods, wild sullen grisly creatures, who, angerly bearded and extravagantly undeterred, brought with them menacingly exotic instruments and, sometimes, wordless ghostly staring children, their fathers keeping to their dismal labors for days without sleep, taking no recesses for food even—greasy oblongs of oil-darkened canvas spread out all about as the place more and more accumulated the inward parts of . . . *our imported piece!*—the thing nauseatingly sundered, the inmost laid open, the hidden laid bare, the genius of the thing suddenly truly charmlessly alien, whatever the truth of its origin.

No help.

Nothing worked.

The clock kept keeping the wrong time.

But no one is saying the clock was ever a stroke less reassuring to look upon.

He who looked upon the clock was reassured.

She, too.

Made present to the wonder of things in being, of no change, of the venerable venerating itself, of nothing giving up in the teeth of everything defeating.

It was okay.

THE CHILDREN HAD COME and gone.

To be sure, the notion of the generations was just beginning to exert itself good and proper the year the couple packed up and gave up the place where the marriage had conducted its offspring into the habits that had been proclaimed for them. So here was the time for something smaller and more manageable, for a dwelling better fitted to the compressions of middle age—and the clock, of course, went to this dwelling with them—all the time in the world for passing such a patrimony along to the first one to wed—no, to the first one to honor the ceremonies of homemaking—oh, but no yet again—to

the first one to express the resolution to prostrate himself and spouse before a token of the household, consent-
ing to welcome unto their destinies the instruction the
clock would give.

BUT, LOOK—see how we, the tellers of what is told,
are not exempt from what is said?

Behold, must not the clock keep perfect time before
the story can claim for itself storyhood?

And so it does!

All day.

Every day.

And all the next ones, too.

MAGIC!

How else to explain but as magic?

The spontaneous institution of what was helplessly
wanted—everything in unimprovable order—nothing
even a tick's tock off.

Go ahead, call the timekeepers in, get in touch with
the lucky custodians, telephone from right in there—we
mean from right in there in the little sleeping room the
widow and I have now taken to storing the clock in and
to keeping tidied and anointed for the visits of our
children's children's children.

You'll see.

Say "Could you please tell me what time it is, please?"

Now watch the clock.

Right on the money, yes?

But here is the thing.

Every time the old woman and I hear it chiming the time it really is, a ridiculous condition of panic takes up our minds in its hand and twists. I mean, the clock, the good old clock—our very index of the durable order of things—has got us scared stiff.

ON THE BUSINESS OF
GENERATING TRANSFORMS

I have, for example,
heard such sentences
as "They didn't know
what each other should do" . . .

—NOAM CHOMSKY

HE DID NOT MEAN IN Ahnenerbe, in Ahmecetka, in Ananiev, in Apion, Arad, Armyansk, Artemovsk, Aumeier, Auschwitz, Baden, Bad Tölz, Baetz, Ballensiefen, Balti, Belzec, Beresovka, Bergen-Belsen, Bessarabia, Birkenau, Blizyn, Bobruisk, Bolzano, Borisov, Borispol, Brabag, Bratislava, Breendonck, Breslau, Brest Litovsk, Buchenwald, Budzyn, Bukovina, Chelmno, Chisinau, Chmiolnik, Chortkov, Cservenka, Czestochowa, Dachau, Dorohoi, Dorohucza, Dubno, Flir, Florstedt, Flossenbürg, Gomel, Gorlitz, Grodno, Hilversum, Kamenka, Karlovac, Karsava, Kaunas, Kharkov, Kirovograd, Kislovodsk, Kistarcsa, Klimovichni, Koblenz, Kobryn, Kodyma, Kopkow, Kowel, Krakow-Placzow, Krzemienec, Kulmhof, Kummer, Kurhessen, Kursk, Kysak, Kyustendil, Langleist, Larissa, Lida, Liscka, Litzenberg, Ljubljana, Lodz, Lom, Lublin, Lvov, Majdanek, Malkinia, Mariupol, Mielec, Mitrovica, Mogilev, Moldavia, Monowitz, Nasielek, Neu-Sandez, Nevel, Novo Moskovsk, Novo Ukrainka, Olshanka, Opitz, Oppeln, Oswiecim, Pionki, Plovdiv, Poltava, Poniatowa, Poznan, Pristina, Pskov, Raschwitz, Ravensbrück, Rawa-Ruska, Regensburg, Rovno, Saarbrucken,

Saarpflaz, Salonika, Sambor, Sdolbunov, Silesia, Simferopol, Skopje, Slavyansk, Slivina, Slovakia, Slovenia, Slutsk, Sluzk, Smolensk, Snigerevka, Snovsk, Sobibor, Sonsken, Struma, Staden, Stammlager, Stettin, Szarva, Szeged, Szolnok-Doboka, Taganrog, Tallin, Târgu-Mures, Tarnopol, Tartu, Theresienstadt, Tighina, Timisoara, Tiraspol, Tizabogdany, Tomaschow, Transnistria, Trawniki, Treblinka, Trikkala, Trzynietz, Turck, Turda, Uzhorod, Vapniarka, Varna, Vijnita, Vilna, Vinnitsa, Vitebsk, Vitezka, Volhynia-Podolia, or in Vyazma, or in Zakopane, or in Zangen, or in Zupp.

But, yes, certainly it is probably true they did not know what each other should do. They probably did not know what even they themselves should.

FISH STORY

AS FAR AS I WAS ALWAYS CONCERNED, the outdoors was where you maybe went when it wasn't raining and only when you had to. I wasn't the only indoorsy type in my parish to cherish this unhealthy opinion. One thing was, you couldn't hear *Jack Armstrong* under some spreading chestnut tree—because Jewish boys did not have spreading chestnut trees and, anyway, back in those backward burnished days, portable radios went about three pounds shy of the total tonnage of the *Normandie*, crew and cargo loaded. Or maybe they hadn't even invented them yet—portable radios, I mean, not Jewish boys. But the days were indeed backward, all right, aglow with the feeble light those ancient flame-shaped amber bulbs struggled to give off. Everybody's mother thought they were the cat's pajamas, those cunning bulbs, just the thing for the fake-Tudor houses everybody lived in. Oh, we were all as happy as clams in those glowy places the mothers tried to pry us from into the bright outdoorsy day calling all unwholesome boys. All you wanted week-days was a box of Uneeda Biscuits and a row of Walnettos, to sustain you from *Jack Armstrong* through *Lorenzo Jones*. Saturdays, *Let's Pretend* and *Grand Central Station* so filled the inner kid and stilled the organs of ingestion, you went serenely, the whole day, without. Sundays we won't even talk about, so you and your loved ones will not have to hear what it sounds like when a grown man sobs. Oh, I suppose I can risk a little bit, mention just *The Shadow*, *The Adventures of Nick Carter—Master Detective*, and *Quick as a Flash,* and leave it, I think, impressively, unbeatably, at that.

Are you kidding me—the outdoors? The outdoors was for droolers and for nose-pickers, for kids called Buster and Butch and the one, I swear, called Bix. The outdoors was for the kid we called "Wedge" because, you know, because someone had told us your wedge was your simplest basic elementary tool.

But sometimes God was merciless and it did not rain.

It was then that the mothers came armed with reminders of Green Harvey, to breach the ramparts and storm the trenches of Bad Hygiene.

But first they'd move into action with rickets.

You'll get rickets!

(Aw, Ma, what's rickets?)

Rickets is *from not playing outdoors and from eating meat from a can! Do I ever give you meat from a can?*

(Aw, Ma, I've got to stay tuned for a coded message.)

Tell me something, Mr. Young-Man-Who-Is-Willing-To-Break-A-Mother's-Blood-Vessel, have you lately taken a good look at Harvey Joel Rosensweig?

Visions of Green Harvey an uncomfortable number of houses away always did the ruthless trick. Because you did not want to look like Harvey Joel Rosensweig anymore than Harvey Joel Rosensweig did. And if you were the sort of chicken-hearted impressionable I was, the mother in question did not have to break a blood vessel. You want to divide a believer from the family Emerson, you will never get a better crowbar than Visions of Green Harvey. But this, of course, was back when liddlies were backward and just little.

Which reminds me of another thing which they had not invented yet—which was smart kids. Not only that, but they also hadn't *un*invented parents who never heard of traumatizing the crap out of a ten-year-old.

Green Harvey!

Jeepers, you never saw a kid quicker when it came to buckling on his swashes.

SO THERE YOU WERE, on the lawn, just crazy to participate in the American Way of Life. You had the Wheaties box to guide you in the modalities of how your American boy is supposed to play, but what you did not have was anybody to do it with—because this was the day it was your mother who was the only mother home to hound her issue into the streets, all of the other mothers being at the neighborhood rummy game, which is where it is mothers and fathers in a perfect world were always meant to be.

I'd sit on the curb for a time and stare at some glinty thing in the gutter. I don't know what it was with me, but in those backward burnished days, whenever I sat on a curb, this is what I would do, cut my eyes sideways from side to side until I had spotted some glittery thing, a bonanza in the gutter. Then I'd sit there, at whatever distance, trying to guess what it was. Not guess, really, but just declare aloud with mad conviction—alone like this, you being Renfrew of the Royal Mounties or Sergeant Preston of the Yukon—the startling powers in you something scary in your solitude. Hey, whatever it was, off there in the gutter, who even needed a second glint?

Gum wrapper!

And then you'd get up and go look.

The time's too backward and burnished for me to remember if I ever did guess right. But I remember one day what it was when the guess I'd guessed was nowhere near to close, which—okay, okay, you got me, okay?—which incident is what accounts for my getting into this whole outdoorsy business with you in the first place.

Because one day it was a fishhook!

NOW A FISHHOOK IN THE GUTTER was not a discovery you routinely made in the gutters of the streets where I come from. I'm talking about a place called the Five Towns, a sort of way-station along the ongoing Diaspora about twenty miles out on Long Island, counting from the center of familial concern—which was where all of the fathers bravely went each day with their brown suits and their fedora hats.

I wasn't all that dumb about fishing, mind you. Not

only did I know it was a thing the Wheaties box okayed, but I knew almost all the grammar-school readers had Skippy always doing it with his dad, or had Bucky always wanting to do it with his pa, or had Franklin Delano Roosevelt telling a story about it to his dog.

I knew they all did it with an animal they called a worm and that they did it with a stick they called a pole. I knew they got a *worm* and a *line* and a *pole,* and that where they went with them to do it was to a *crick.*

I wasn't too sure we had anything around there where we lived which would qualify as a crick, but the first three items I figured for a cinch. Hook in hand—you know, *holding* it—my mother's shrieked philosophy conjuring in my mind's ear the shout of calamity (*You will put an eye out with that thing!*), I headed for the garage, happy to be in darkness for the time it would take for me to get the pole (a piece of picket fence, an upright left over because the lawn we had did not go that far) and the line (a bunch of Venetian-blind cord the vermin had set up for themselves as a haven in a heartless world).

Worm.

Worm?

I'd seen a few in my time—but not really where they had come from. I mean, a worm was something Green Harvey would come running at you with—until you had had the luck to see him coming and the good sense for you to take off a safe distance the other way, far enough for his fat to make Green Harvey quit coming and eat it—the worm. But it never crossed my mind to wonder where Harvey Joel Rosensweig got his worm from. I suppose I just leaped to the conclusion you had to be a Harvey Joel Rosensweig to get one.

Worm! Worm! Worm!

I think I remember scuffing up the pebbles in our driveway for a trice or two, giving many maddening seconds to my idea of how a real American boy breasts all hardship to quest the Great Quest. What I mean is I was by this time back in those backward burnished days pretty damn wised-up as to a pessimist's construction of everything in sight—meaning: if I did not catch a fish, I would be the last one to be surprised. Listen, it was a boyhood perpendicular to the kind you read about in the readers in school. It was a boyhood where the community never rested in its preparations for disaster and was amazed, seemed disappointed, when it did not strike. It was a boyhood where standards were sky-high but where expectation had been leached out of them to make for you a non-annihilating semi-null class. Come on, I'm not whining—I am just giving you the whole heart-rending tragic picture.

SO HERE WE ARE, nostalgia fans, back behind the family garage with a piece of picket fence, about nine feet of chewed-up Venetian-blind cord, and a hook Satan had set out to do temptation's work there in a gutter-looker's gutter. But you're thinking crick, you're thinking where does the kid get a crick from? Well, it takes the kid about a half hour to walk it to the crick, an inlet (let in by the Atlantic Ocean) spanned by a little bridge you crossed to get to the beach clubs. We called this inlet The Inlet, and we called the bridge The Bridge—not unmindful of how Skippy and Bucky were always coming up with these really great names for things—it dawning on me that if you got yourself out there on a little poke of dock up on out there on the landward side (hello, Skippy! hello, Bucky!), you could drop a line down into something maybe liquid and deep enough.

Look, I can appreciate how knot-tying is probably a pretty big deal to most people, but for me there's never been much in it for me after the shoelace stage. So if you are wondering how I got the Venetian-blind cord stuck onto the piece of picket fence, do me a favor and save your worry for the hook.

Because the hook, jeez, the hook truly was a bitch. I mean, I tried a lot of very fancy thinking, but my brain could only handle in my mind the mental thought it definitely, the hook, could not be done.

So I just dropped the line in, tossed the Venetian-blind cord in, hookless but serious-looking if you went by the principle of its having lifted up its share of slats.

YOU READY?

You're ready!

Because how else could this all come out but as a good and countervailing lesson for a boy who always waited for the worst?

I am not saying what happened converted an indoors type to an outdoors one. Please, I still get closest to God somewhere where you can control the light. All I am saying is I went ahead and pulled up no fewer than a dozen lunatic fish with that stick of picket fence—fish which just bit anywhere all at once on that Venetian-blind cord and which looked like they were not going to let go of it wherever they'd bit on a bet.

I did not take even one of them home to prove it, though. As a matter of fact, I did not try to yank even one of them off the line. I just dropped the stick and ran like hell, all twelve or so of those infectious things on there fastened to it for good.

You know who would have stuck around?

I bet you Green Harvey would have stuck around— the loon probably harvesting those evil-minded monstrosities just to pitch one through the window of every mother's son who ever had believed himself to be far enough away from any undoing indoors.

But me, I had had my fair warning of what is sometimes under outdoor things.

Knew I'd never need to know more.

IT WAS BETTER THAN THIRTY YEARS LATER, when I was turning the pages of a Ladybird Book for an indoorsy type of my own (a kid whose peaceable opinion of nature continues to treacherously thrive on an abundance of urban ignorance), that I found out what it was the Wheaties box had got me into back in the backward burnished days when my heart was brave and true—namely, the worst scare ever to chase me through all of the backward burnish of my youth.

It was just a blowfish.

They were just blowfish.

Every last one of them a blown-up certitude in and of itself.

Oh, it will bite on any fool thing, your natural blowfish will. But so, for that matter—hook, line, and sinker—will your friendly reader. I mean, since it is all the same in the end, and if it is all the same to you, give me human nature every time—and the equally metaphoric, equally dubious, equally muddled angling of men.